She couldn't see him...

But the bedroom air stirred. Then she felt his kiss, a butterfly kiss, on her lips. A caress that tantalized her senses, that made her capable of nothing else but returning his kiss.

It was as though he knew her, how to tease her, how to please her. "Troy?" Bree whispered. But he remained silent, never stopping, drawing her into his sensual spell.

Deep inside she felt doubt stirring. Whether this man was Troy or not, he had come to her without announcing his name or his intentions. He'd come to her bed like a phantom lover.

Her eyes flew open. She couldn't see him, but she pushed him away. For a millisecond she felt the resistance of warm flesh, of muscle and bone. Then her hands pressed upward through chilled, empty air.

He was gone. Vanished, as silently and as swiftly as he had come to her.

Dear Harlequin Intrigue Reader,

This month Harlequin Intrigue has a healthy dose of breathtaking romantic suspense to reignite you after the cold winter days. Kicking things off, Susan Kearney delivers the first title in her brand-new trilogy HEROES INC., based on a specially trained team of sexy agents taking on impossible missions. In *Daddy to the Rescue,* an operative is dispatched to safeguard his ex-wife from the danger that threatens her. Only, now he also has to find the child she claims is his!

Rebecca York returns with the latest installment in her hugely popular 43 LIGHT STREET series. *Phantom Lover* is a supersexy gothic tale of suspense guaranteed to give you all kinds of fantasies.... Also appearing this month is another veteran Harlequin Intrigue author, Patricia Rosemoor, with the next title in her CLUB UNDERCOVER miniseries. In *VIP Protector,* a bodyguard must defend a prominent attorney from a crazed stalker. But can he protect her from long-buried secrets best left hidden?

Finally rounding out the month is the companion title in our MEN ON A MISSION theme promotion, *Tough as Nails,* from debut author Jackie Manning. Here an estranged couple must join forces to solve a deadly mystery, but will their close proximity fuel the flames of passion smoldering between them?

So pick up all four of these thrilling, action-packed stories for a full course of unbelievable excitement!

Sincerely,

Denise O'Sullivan
Senior Editor
Harlequin Intrigue

PHANTOM LOVER

REBECCA YORK

RUTH GLICK WRITING AS REBECCA YORK

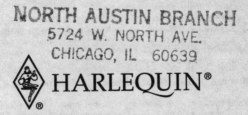

HARLEQUIN®

TORONTO • NEW YORK • LONDON
AMSTERDAM • PARIS • SYDNEY • HAMBURG
STOCKHOLM • ATHENS • TOKYO • MILAN • MADRID
PRAGUE • WARSAW • BUDAPEST • AUCKLAND

ISBN 0-373-22706-X

PHANTOM LOVER

Copyright © 2003 by Ruth Glick

This edition published by arrangement with Harlequin Books S.A.

® and TM are trademarks of the publisher. Trademarks indicated with ® are registered in the United States Patent and Trademark Office, the Canadian Trade Marks Office and in other countries.

Visit us at www.eHarlequin.com

Printed in U.S.A.

ABOUT THE AUTHOR

Award-winning, bestselling novelist Ruth Glick, who writes as Rebecca York, is the author of close to eighty books, including her popular 43 LIGHT STREET series for Harlequin Intrigue. Ruth says she has the best job in the world. Not only does she get paid for telling stories; she's also the author of twelve cookbooks. Ruth and her husband, Norman, travel frequently, researching locales for her novels and searching out new dishes for her cookbooks.

Books by Rebecca York

HARLEQUIN INTRIGUE

*43 Light Street
**43 Light Street/Mine To Keep
†Peregrine Connection

Don't miss any of our special offers. Write to us at the following address for information on our newest releases.

Harlequin Reader Service
U.S.: 3010 Walden Ave., P.O. Box 1325, Buffalo, NY 14269
Canadian: P.O. Box 609, Fort Erie, Ont. L2A 5X3

Dear Reader,

In *Phantom Lover* I wanted to write a novel with all the classic gothic trappings. You know how a gothic tale starts. A naive young woman comes to an isolated estate to be the governess of a young child. She's immediately immersed in a world of secrets and intrigue, a world where nothing is as it seems—and the master of the house is a dark, brooding man with deep emotional wounds. Yet his sexual attraction for the heroine is powerful. Can she trust him? Should she surrender to him? Can her love save his soul?

I had a wonderful time playing with these themes, and I pushed them to their limits. My isolated estate is called Ravencrest. In my story that dark, brooding hero, Troy London, may be a ghost. Or is he? That's something you'll have to decide for yourself.

There are a couple of the classic elements that I did bend in my story. I love to write a sensual book, and this one is no exception. Troy London wants Bree, and he uses all his considerable skill as a lover to get what he wants. And then there's my heroine. She's smart enough to bring a gun along with her to Ravencrest. But she simply couldn't calculate the risks she'd be taking by setting foot on the estate.

Enjoy!

Ruth

Ruth Glick writing as Rebecca York

CAST OF CHARACTERS

Troy London—Was he dead or alive? Desperate or calculating?

Bree Brennan—Could she save the man she loved? Was he worth saving?

Helen London—She was sending Bree into a dangerous situation.

Dinah London—Had Troy's daughter seen her father recently, or was she telling stories?

Nola Sterling—Why was she giving Bree a hard time?

Abner Sterling—Was Nola's husband dangerous or deranged? Or both?

Foster Graves—Was he just the handyman—or a major player in the drama unfolding at Ravencrest?

Edith Martindale—Was she an ally or an enemy?

Miss Carpenter—Did the former schoolteacher get fired, or was she scared into quitting?

Prologue

Troy London squinted against the wind blowing salt spray into his face and matting the dark hair to his forehead. Tipping back his head, he looked up to the cliffs at the great house towering above the ocean.

Ravencrest. The estate his great-grandfather had built. For the first time in months he felt the joy of coming home to this place. Well, a muted joy, with the present problems hanging over him. But he would solve them— one way or the other. And then he'd get his life back on track again.

Deftly he maneuvered the small craft through the swells, finding the calm channel between the towering rocks.

He had sailed these waters since he was a boy. For sport and for the challenge of pitting his mind and body against the elements.

He found the ring anchored to the rock and tied up the boat, then waited for a swell to crest before stepping off onto the landing platform, slippery with ocean water. Using the familiar handholds, he climbed the rough-hewn steps toward the top of the cliff.

He could have approached the house from the headlands. But then he would be visible from the west-facing windows. Instead, he stopped at the entrance to one of the secret tunnels carved into the stone. Opening the door, he slipped into a dark passage.

A flashlight was hanging from the wall, and he used it to guide his way up a steep slope and then more stairs.

At breakfast he'd announced his intention to go sailing. He'd made sure they saw him heading out into the ocean. But he'd come back sooner than they expected, hugging the coast to keep from being spotted.

And now perhaps he could get the evidence he needed, because he wouldn't act without proof.

A sick feeling overtook him. It was tinged with his own guilt—over what he'd done and what he hadn't done, if the truth be told.

Still, he'd expected better than this, and he'd thought long and hard about what to do. He was still hoping he was mistaken. Hoping against hope that he'd read all the signals wrong.

Stopping at a fork in the passage, he listened intently, then moved silent as a panther toward one of the rooms.

He'd laid a trap there the day before. Now he would see what he had caught.

He set down the flashlight, then pressed on a hidden panel and stepped into the back of a closet. Slowly he opened the door, just enough to see into the room. The man was there, just as he'd suspected, just as he'd feared.

"What are you doing?" he asked, keeping his voice low and steady as he walked into the room.

The man's eyes widened. "Where did you come from?"

"That's not important. Answer my question." He walked forward, his gaze focused on the interloper, so that he didn't see that another person was standing in the bathroom.

At the last second a flash of movement caught the corner of his eye and he realized his mistake. But it was too late. The blow came crashing down on his head. And then there was only blackness.

Chapter One

Fog rolled in from the west, obscuring the rugged coast-line north of San Francisco. There was no guardrail, the narrow stretch of road was slick, and Bree Brennan slowed her rental car, thinking that if she plunged into the ocean, it would be her own damn fault.

She'd been acting recklessly when she'd taken a leave of absence from the Light Street Detective Agency. She was still acting recklessly. The new Bree Brennan, she thought with a mental shake of her head. When she'd joined the agency two years ago, she'd been Bonnie. Now she was Bree—a different person. More daring. More in charge of her life. At least in her own eyes.

Only the farther she'd come along California Highway One, the more second thoughts she'd had. Her old persona whispered in her head that she should turn around and go home. But she simply couldn't do it. She'd be letting down a lot of people, including the new Bree Brennan. And her friend Helen London.

When a shaft of lightning shattered the darkening sky, Bree responded with a quavery laugh. If she'd been the director of a horror movie, she couldn't have done a bet-ter job of setting the scene: the naive young woman driving through the storm toward a spooky old mansion. Except this was no movie. It was real life.

Helen's distraught phone call from Macedonia echoed in her mind.

"I'm so scared. I'm afraid Troy is dead. I haven't talked to him in two weeks. And his e-mails are really strange—like somebody else is writing them for him."

She was talking about her older brother, Troy London, both of them named by an eccentric father with a passion for Greek literature.

Bree had gotten to know Troy seven years earlier when she'd been visiting the Londons' summer place—their ranch in Montana. She'd been attracted to him, and she'd thought the attraction was mutual. Then she'd been called away abruptly to take care of problems at home. Once she was back in her own environment, she'd told herself a relationship with Troy wouldn't have worked anyway. He came from a world of wealth and privilege, so different from her own background.

Still, she'd never let go of the memories of a virile, vibrant young man with dark hair, warm hazel eyes and a ready smile.

Like his sister, he didn't need to work, but both siblings had wanted meaningful jobs. Helen was a Foreign Service Officer. Troy had specialized in taking failing companies, turning them around and selling them at a profit. He'd had exactly the life he wanted, until a year ago when his wife had been killed in a car accident and he had shut himself away at Ravencrest, his estate on the northern California coast.

Bree slammed on her brakes as another fork of lightning split the sky directly in front of her, illuminating the entrance to the property. Great timing, she thought as she turned in at the access road. Ravencrest was one of the few large tracts of property left along the coast. Most of the big estates had been subdivided or turned into parks and other public access areas. But Ravencrest was a throwback to another era.

In a fast and furious exchange of e-mail, after their initial phone conversation, she and Helen had cooked up a plan to get Bree into the house—a plan that would keep her here while she found out what was going on. It had made sense back in Baltimore. Now...

Now she was dead tired and full of doubts. She'd gotten up at the crack of dawn, changed planes twice and driven a hundred and fifty miles along these winding, narrow roads. She was in no shape to sound brilliant. But there was no way to avoid the coming confrontation.

Pulling up in front of the iron gate, she rolled down her window, pressed the button on the intercom and looked up toward the television camera focused on her window.

Long, nerve-racking seconds passed before a woman's voice asked, "Yes? Who is it?"

It sounded like an older woman. Probably the housekeeper, Edith Martindale, whom Helen had described to Bree. Good. Mrs. Martindale probably wasn't going to be as tough a gatekeeper as one of the Sterlings, the distant relatives who had moved in with Troy two months ago.

"I'm Bree Brennan," she answered, exaggerating her native North Carolina accent so that her name came out as a thick, honeyed drawl. "I'm Dinah London's new teacher," she added, very glad that she'd taught first grade for the Baltimore County schools before joining the Light Street Detective Agency.

There was a hesitation on the other end of the line. "I didn't know Mrs. Sterling hired a teacher for Dinah."

Mrs. Sterling was Nola Sterling. She and her husband, Abner, were supposed to be down on their luck, which was why Troy had allowed them to move into Ravencrest. According to Helen, they'd taken over the place.

Bree dragged a deep breath and held it for a second before answering with a complete non sequitur. "I've driven all the way up here from San Francisco, and I can't go back tonight."

"Well…"

Bree went on quickly. "I was hired by Helen London when she learned that her niece's previous instructor, Miss Carpenter, had been dismissed."

"Ms. London is out of the country. How could she hire you?"

"Didn't she send you a message?"

Again there was that slight hesitation. "No. I don't think so."

Probably the housekeeper was wondering if Nola Sterling had neglected to inform her of the new arrangement. That would make sense, but in fact, Bree and Helen had decided that making her arrival a surprise was the best plan. And Helen had arranged not to be available.

Following their script she said, "She interviewed me by e-mail. And she sent me an authorization by fax." As she spoke, she pulled out the paper and held it up to the camera.

After half a minute she lowered the fax and stared into the camera again, her blue eyes wide and naive. "Whom am I speaking to?" she asked politely.

"Mrs. Martindale," the woman confirmed.

"Is Mr. London there?"

"He's not available at the moment."

Through the television camera, she felt herself being

scrutinized and kept her own gaze steady. Her appearance was a plus, she knew.

Around the Light Street office, she always looked businesslike. But it didn't take much effort to transform herself into the classic subject of a dumb blond joke. She'd combed her shoulder-length wheat-colored hair to frame her face in soft waves and carefully outlined her bow-shaped lips. And now she kept her blue eyes wide, as though she'd just walked off the farm.

"Come up to the house." As the woman spoke, the gate creaked open.

With a sigh that was part relief and part trepidation, Bree drove through. As the barrier clanked shut behind her, she couldn't help feeling like an inmate arriving at prison.

Hands clamped to the wheel, she steered the car up the winding drive, past pine trees dripping with green moss that fluttered in the wind blowing off the ocean.

Now that she was here, it was hard to catch her breath, and she knew she had good reason to be edgy. When Helen had first contacted her, Bree had proposed that one of the men from the Light Street Detective Agency or Randolph Security, which worked closely with them, should find out what was wrong at Ravencrest.

Her friend had argued against that plan. "The Sterlings are up to something bad. I just know it. If they think they're being attacked or investigated, they could take Dinah hostage. Maybe they've already done it—to keep Troy in line. They could have him locked up somewhere. Or maybe they have him drugged. Or he might already be dead. And if they've killed him, what would stop them from killing his daughter?"

Helen had always had a flair for the dramatic.

"Those are pretty serious accusations," Bree had said

carefully. "You think your cousins are capable of something like that? What would their motive be?"

"I don't know. I've never even met them. I don't think Troy had, either, before they showed up." She sighed. "Probably I sound hysterical. But I'm so frightened. Before Grace died, I never worried about Troy. But he turned so spacy." She sighed. "If I could take care of this myself, I would."

If the plea for help had come from anybody else, Bree wouldn't be here now. But five years ago, when her mother had needed a kidney transplant, Helen had loaned her the money for the operation. They'd worked out a payment plan, but when Bree had sent the first check, Helen had refused to accept it. Mom had lived three more years after that. And Bree knew that Helen had given her those years. Which was why Bree had gone off to Northern California, without giving anybody at the Light Street Detective Agency a chance to point out all the flaws in her plan.

The impending storm had darkened the sky so that it might as well have been midnight. As she rounded a curve in the drive, lightning illuminated the outline of what looked like a stone fortress. It was almost as though some supernatural force was directing her attention to the house.

Helen had described it as a cross between a medieval castle and a Disney fantasy, built by a great-grandfather, Cecil London, who had made his money in some undisclosed business. Designed as a grand statement of his wealth, it had always given Helen the creeps. But Troy had been charmed by the place. When the estate had been passed to them, Troy had enthusiastically moved in with his wife, Grace, and together they'd started the monumental job of remodeling.

Then Grace had died and Troy had lost interest in life. Well, not everything in life, Helen had said. He'd still been devoted to his six-year-old daughter.

Mist swirled over the road, adding to the sense that Bree was driving into a scene from a horror movie. The old house rose out of the fog, a man-made chunk of rock dominating the darkening skyline.

The long lane was hemmed in by overgrown shrubbery. As she reached the circular drive, the rain finally broke, a burst like machine gun bullets hitting the car roof.

Pulling forward, she was relieved to discover that she could find shelter under a large covered porch. After releasing the trunk latch, she stepped out onto paving bricks, hearing the rain drumming on the roof and feeling a blast of cold air whipping at her hair.

Resolutely, she tried to keep her gaze within the lighted area under the porch, but the foliage swaying in the wind teased the edges of her vision and prickled the hairs on the back of her neck.

"You're spooked by this place, and you're not even inside yet," she muttered, just to hear the sound of her own voice.

Walking to the trunk, she leaned in to retrieve the suitcase. As she pulled it out, she felt a large, warm hand press down on her shoulder.

The touch was so totally unexpected that she screamed. When she whirled to confront the jerk who had snuck up in back of her, there was nobody in sight.

Blinking, she stared into empty space. She was sure she wasn't mistaken. Somebody had cupped his hand possessively over her shoulder. A man, judging by the weight and size of the touch. Then, before she could turn around, he'd disappeared into the swaying shrubbery.

And she was left with the faint scent of spicy aftershave dissipating on the wind.

The shiver that had started at the back of her neck worked its way down her spine as she tried to probe the darkness beyond the lighted entrance.

For several moments she stood beside the open trunk, taking shallow, even breaths, wondering if her imagination was running away with her and thinking she should pull out the jack handle to use as a weapon.

Finally she picked up her suitcase, slammed the trunk shut and marched toward the massive stone facade of the building. She had lifted her hand to knock on the wide wooden door when it suddenly opened, throwing her off balance.

The doorway was broad, and her hand missed the jamb as she made a frantic grab to steady herself. Despite her best efforts to stop her forward motion, she stumbled several paces across a marble floor into a rectangular reception area.

The ploy had been deliberate and nasty, to make her land on her face. But she kept her footing, set down her suitcase with a thunk and straightened. As she lifted her head she found herself facing a tall, thin woman wearing black slacks and a black blouse. She was standing with her arms folded tightly in front of her.

She appeared to be in her mid-forties, with short brown hair threaded with gray strands. Her face was long and angular, and her dark eyes focused on Bree as though she were studying an insect that had crawled under the door.

"Mrs. Martindale told me you were on your way up here, of all things! What took you so long getting from the gate to the house?"

"In this weather I was driving cautiously," Bree responded. Then she asked, "Are you Mrs. Sterling?"

"Yes. Did you see anything strange?"

Bree waited a beat then asked, "What do you mean, exactly?"

Mrs. Sterling shrugged. "I simply want your impressions."

"Well, the drive is kind of spooky in the dark, with the fog rolling in."

The woman gave a curt nod, her lips pressed together, her eyes unnerving as they remained pinned on her unexpected guest.

Trying to ignore the unpleasant sensation, Bree deliberately changed the focus of her gaze, looking around at the antique furniture, then craned her neck upward so she could take in the crystal chandelier.

"Oh, it's so good to get inside. This place is so lovely," she gushed, drawling out the syllables like Scarlett O'Hara on her best behavior.

"Before you make yourself at home, let me see that fax from Helen London," Mrs. Sterling snapped, still not bothering with polite pleasantries such as, "Hello. How are you?"

Pretending not to notice the rudeness, Bree bent, hiding her face as she opened her purse and produced the paper. She was badly off balance, but she was determined not to let it show.

Her unwilling hostess took the fax to an elaborately carved side table and thrust the paper under the light cast by a small Tiffany lamp.

After reading through the authorization she demanded, "And your ID. I'd like to make sure you're who you say you are."

Bree's heart was still thumping in her chest, but she calmly pulled out her wallet and extracted her driver's license, which got the same treatment as the fax.

With a scowl, Mrs. Sterling handed them both back. "So is your name Bonnie or Bree?"

"Bree is my legal name now. I haven't gotten around to changing my license."

"Why the switch?"

"Bonnie is so old-fashioned," she drawled. "Bree is so much more charming."

"If you want to sound like a piece of French cheese."

Bree blinked, wondering how to respond. But Mrs. Sterling was still speaking.

"Yes, well, it's inconvenient that I can't pick up the phone and call Ms. London. As I understand it, she's off on a special assignment and out of contact with the civilized world. Did she say why she has the authorization to hire a teacher?"

Bree put on her best innocent face. "I'm so sorry if I've stepped into an awkward situation. I just hate to be a bother." She stopped and fluttered her hands. "She mentioned that Dinah has always been home-schooled. And since her mother died—" She stopped and gestured helplessly again. "Since her mother died, teachers have taken over the job. But Ms. London seemed concerned about her niece. I mean, she said that her brother had been, uh, wallowing in grief over his wife's death, and he hadn't been paying adequate attention to his daughter's welfare. So if he wasn't going to hire a new teacher, she was going to do it for him." She stopped abruptly, looking like she was surprised to have delivered such a long speech.

"This is highly irregular."

Bree's only reply was a helpless look. She was relieved of the obligation to answer when Mrs. Sterling's gaze suddenly shot to the hallway on the left. "Dinah, come out here!'' the woman demanded. ''How many times have I told you not to sneak around?''

Several seconds passed before a little girl stepped out from behind a display case and walked slowly into the entrance hall, stopping several paces from the adults.

Helen had told her Dinah was six. She looked younger, small and fragile with huge, pale eyes, pale skin and a riot of unruly chestnut curls falling around her shoulders.

It wasn't difficult for Bree to imagine her in a long Edwardian dress, but the girl was wearing more prosaic blue jeans and a light yellow T-shirt. One arm was held stiffly at her side. The other cradled a fuzzy stuffed animal, its identity hidden by the girl's close embrace.

Lifting her head, she looked toward Bree, her expression expectant. ''You're my new teacher,'' she said in a low voice.

''Yes. How did you know?''

''Daddy told me you were coming. So I've been waiting for you.'' The small, wistful voice made Bree's heart squeeze.

Mrs. Sterling's face contorted. ''He couldn't have said that! *I* didn't even know she was coming.''

Dinah gave a small, dismissive shrug. ''He's smart. He knows things you don't.''

The woman in black stared at the child, apparently struggling for a response. Then she imitated Dinah's shrug. ''Have it your way,'' she snapped. ''I think you're lying. I think you heard us talking just now.''

Bree tried to work her way through the exchange, the spoken part and the subtext. Helen had told her that Dinah was a very clever, very imaginative child. Was she making up the conversation with her father? Or was Troy London being held captive somewhere and Nola Sterling was angry that Dinah had managed to talk to him?

Putting her own questions aside, Bree knelt so that she was at the little girl's eye level. "My name is Bree Brennan," she said, holding out her hand. "And I'm very glad I'm going to be your teacher."

Her face grave, Dinah extended her free arm, and they shook.

"Who's your friend?" Bree asked.

"Alice."

"Can I see her?"

After a short hesitation Dinah freed the stuffed toy and held it out. Bree saw gray and white fur, pointed ears and button eyes. The fur was slightly matted and worn, as though the child had been clutching the animal over a long period of time.

Like a security blanket, Bree thought with a pang. She heard the child's voice quaver slightly as she said, "Alice is a kitty."

"Yes."

Mrs. Sterling interrupted the exchange with strident words to Bree. "My husband and I eat quite late—too late for the little girl. I'm sure Dinah will be glad to show you to your quarters—and have your company at dinner in the schoolroom."

Her quarters? Was she expected to sleep in the servants' wing? Bree wondered as she stood again.

The woman turned to Dinah and issued an imperious order. "Take her upstairs."

Under ordinary circumstances, Bree would have vetoed giving such duties to a child. But she was glad she and Dinah were going to be alone soon. That would give them a chance to get acquainted. And they could talk in the schoolroom tomorrow.

If the schoolroom wasn't bugged. As that thought flitted into her mind she almost laughed. The idea of a bug in a six-year-old girl's classroom was pretty farfetched. Yet the laugh died before it reached her lips.

She knew that when the guys from the Light Street Detective Agency went into a covert surveillance situation, they were always prepared for bugs. And she'd better remember that things could be similar here. Helen had sent her to Ravencrest because neither one of them knew what the Sterlings had done, and what they might do to protect their position.

Before she had time to consider the possibilities, she heard a door slam, then heavy footsteps pounding down the hall.

Troy?

The child's face went white.

A look of mixed fear and exasperation plastered itself across Nola Sterling's features.

All eyes, Bree's included, focused on the hallway.

Seconds later, a man burst into the foyer, a man whose face was flushed and whose glaring gaze lit on Bree.

Chapter Two

The man stood with his hands balled into fists and his arms bent, like a street fighter ready to take on a crowd. His hands were large—large enough to have created the pressure she remembered on her shoulder. The thought of his having touched her made Bree's stomach knot. Yet it couldn't be him, she told herself. He didn't smell right. His body gave off the scent of sweat, not clean aftershave.

Dinah cringed against her, and she slung her arm around the girl's shoulders, holding her protectively against her side.

"I was doing my regular check of the grounds, and I saw a car out front," he bellowed. Still looking at Bree, he demanded, "Who are you? And what are you doing here?"

"I'm Bree Brennan, Dinah's new teacher." She repeated the information she'd already given several times since arriving, letting her voice slur into a soft drawl.

The tactic didn't have any effect on the man. "Says who?" he demanded.

"Says Helen London," Bree answered, striving to sound a good deal more confident than she was feeling.

"I believe she's still part owner of the property with her brother, Troy," she added for good measure.

The man's mouth opened, then closed again as he apparently thought better of his outburst. It seemed the London name still functioned as some kind of deterrent.

Bree raised her chin and blinked her large blue eyes. "Do I have the pleasure of addressing Abner Sterling?"

"Yes, and don't get smart with me, missy," he snapped.

"That certainly wasn't my intention, sir," she replied.

The fiftyish man looked her up and down, from her damp blond hair to the red slingbacks she'd picked to go with her navy slacks and beige knit top. "You don't look much like a teacher," he said.

She spread her hands and drawled, "I'm hoping you'll find me satisfactory. I came all the way from Baltimore to teach Dinah. She's such a lovely little girl, and I'm sure we're going to get along famously."

"How do you know she's lovely? You just got here," Abner pointed out. "I'm betting you change your opinion after you've been here a little while. She drove the last teacher away, and she'll drive you away, too."

"No, I didn't," Dinah protested.

"That's enough out of you."

The child cringed, and Bree wanted to spring across the space separating her from Abner Sterling and belt him. But she stayed where she was, since she didn't want to get tossed out the door.

"So let's go find my room," she said to Dinah.

The girl nodded solemnly, putting on a burst of speed as she crossed in front of the Sterlings.

What must it be like to live with these people? Bree wondered. Nola was cold, brittle and hostile. Abner was belligerent and probably stupid, although she knew it would be dangerous to underestimate him.

As the girl started up the stairs, Bree picked up her bag and followed, her heels clicking smartly on the marble.

Glancing back at the Sterlings, she said, "Well, good night. I'll see you in the morning. I assume you don't have breakfast too early for Dinah."

She caught up with the child at the top of the steps and they started down a wide, dimly lit hall. For the first fifty feet the paint and carpet looked new and expensive. After turning a corner, they were suddenly walking on worn boards, between gray, dingy walls.

Several paces along the uncarpeted hallway, they turned another corner. Behind her, Bree heard a floorboard creak, and the skin on the back of her neck tingled.

Was Abner Sterling behind her ready to attack? Stopping, she whirled, only to confront a tall, gaunt man who glared at her. His face was lined with vertical wrinkles, but he stood with shoulders squared. His clothing was scruffy—a dark wool jacket, a dirty shirt, blotched pants.

Feeling a sudden pressure against her side, Bree looked down to see that Dinah had also turned and was squeezed very close to her, her free arm still clutching the stuffed kitten. Obviously she, too, was alarmed by the newcomer.

The man ignored the child, his deadly gaze fixed on Bree.

"Who are you? And what are you doing here?" he demanded, his voice low and raspy.

The questions were starting to get tiresome, she thought. "Dinah's new teacher," she answered. "Who are you?"

"Foster Graves." He kept his gaze steady, his stance rigid.

"You work here?"

"I take care of some things, yeah" was his cryptic reply.

Beside her, Dinah stirred.

Bree bent to the child. "Are you all right?" she questioned.

"I don't want to stay here," the little girl whispered.

"We won't."

The child made a small sound, her eyes going wide. Bree turned again, following her gaze, and discovered that Graves had vanished as quickly as he had appeared.

She took several steps down the hall, trying to figure out how he'd managed such a quick escape. Like the man outside in the driveway!

Only now they were inside. Which probably meant he'd stepped into one of the secret passages built into the house—passages that the London children had discovered when they were kids.

She was just reaching for a curtain covering the wall, when Dinah's fingers closed around the fabric of her slacks. "Don't go look for him," she begged. "He's scary. Come see your room."

Although Bree wanted to find out exactly how the man had disappeared so quickly, the child was more important.

"Okay," she agreed, and heard Dinah's small sigh of relief.

The girl led her down another hallway that turned off to the right. Bree was thinking that perhaps she should have left a trail of bread crumbs so she could find her way back downstairs when Dinah stopped in front of a closed door. "This was Miss Carpenter's room. I guess you're supposed to sleep here."

"That sounds right."

Bree turned the knob and pushed the door open, wincing as it creaked on worn hinges. Fumbling along the wall for the light switch, she found it and flipped the toggle, turning on an elaborate, old-fashioned metal-and-glass ceiling fixture.

The rest of the room looked as though it had been redecorated with a combination of new fabrics, gleaming white woodwork and beautifully restored antiques. Under a flowered Oriental rug, the wood floor was newly refinished. And the small green-and-white checks on the bedspread matched the gracefully flowing draperies. The dresser and high chest were polished oak.

"It's nice," she murmured, then crossed the room and laid her suitcase on the double bed.

Dinah gave her a small smile. "I'm glad you like it."

"Did Miss Carpenter like it?" Bree asked.

The girl considered the question. "She did at first, then she said it was spooky."

"Oh."

"I think that's why she left. It didn't have anything to do with me," she added quickly.

"I didn't think so," Bree agreed, even as she digested the new information. Had Miss Carpenter made the decision to leave because she was afraid to stay at Ravencrest? Or had the Sterlings sent her packing?

In this unfamiliar environment, inconvenient questions were piling up like unpaid bills, and it was impossible not to feel overwhelmed. Bree was in over her head and she'd been here less than an hour.

Suddenly unsteady on her feet, she reached to brace her hand against the bedpost, her fingers closing around the carved wood. She'd set her alarm for four in the morning to get through airport security and catch her flight. Now she was jet-lagged, stressed and worn out.

Although she desperately wanted to make friends with Dinah, she was afraid that if she tried to do it in her present condition, she was going to make some crucial mistake that would set the wrong tone for their whole relationship.

Keeping her voice even, she turned toward the girl. "I've had a really long day and I don't think I'm going to be very good company tonight. Would you mind very much if I just go to bed, and we start off fresh in the morning?"

Dinah looked down, dragging her foot in a small half circle over the rug.

Bree felt her heart squeeze as she watched. "I'm probably disappointing you," she said. "I've just gotten here, and you want to get to know me."

Dinah hesitated for several seconds, then gave a small nod.

"Well, I'm really eager to get to know you and Alice, too. But I'd probably fall asleep as soon as I sat down in a chair."

"I understand," the child answered, sounding much older than her years, and Bree had the feeling she'd learned some strategic coping skills in the past few months.

"We can see each other at breakfast. I'm looking forward to that," Bree added, using her last store of energy to sound enthusiastic. Then another thought struck her. "That Mr. Graves—you're not afraid he's going to be in the hall, are you? Do you want me to walk you to your room?"

"No. He never stays up here long."

"That's good."

Dinah hesitated for a moment. "You don't have to worry about me, because my daddy takes care of me."

Bree held back any reaction. "So your daddy's okay? Can I talk to him?"

"Only if he wants you to." Perhaps to forestall more questions, the child darted from the room, and Bree was left staring at the closed door.

What did Dinah's assurance mean? Maybe Troy wasn't a captive, after all. Maybe he was in hiding, watching out for Dinah. Or had the little girl made it all up?

Her hand closed around the door frame to keep herself from running after the girl. She wanted answers, but at the same time, this child tugged at her heartstrings. It was a little girl a lot like Dinah who had started Bonnie Brennan on the road to her new life. She'd been a timid, guarded person when she'd been teaching in Baltimore. Now she realized that teaching had been a safe place for her—where she could deal with children instead of adults. But one afternoon just as class was letting out, a man named Harvey Milner had stormed into the room and demanded that she turn his child, Cathy, over to him. Only Bonnie knew from conversations with his ex-wife that the father didn't even have visitation rights and that he'd threatened to take the girl and flee the state.

Milner's aggressive tactics had scared her, but she'd taken Cathy in her arms and marched down the hall to the principal's office, the angry father trailing behind her, shouting threats.

Afterward she'd been amazed at what she'd done. It had made her see herself in a different light, made her realize that she'd been selling herself short. But still, she hadn't figured out what she'd wanted to do with the rest of her life until she'd read about a kidnapping case in the *Baltimore Sun,* a kidnapping thwarted by the Light Street Detective Agency.

Excitement coursed through her as she'd read the article. And she'd known she'd wanted to work for that agency. She wanted to help other children, and adults. As soon as the school year was over, she'd contacted them. They'd needed a new secretary and were willing to hire her for that job and to start training her to be a lot more than that.

She'd learned a great deal in the past two years— enough to know that she was now way over her head.

Her mouth twisted as she crossed the room on unsteady legs to lock the door. Then she turned around to study her surroundings. Besides the entrance from the hall, there were two other doors—one on the wall opposite the bed and one at the back of the room. She tried the closer one first and found a dark, cavernous closet.

The other led to an opulent bathroom. The idea of soaking her tired muscles in the deep, claw-footed tub was suddenly very appealing. But afraid that if she lay down in hot water, she'd fall asleep, she settled for a quick shower.

After drying off, she pulled on a simple cotton nightgown. In the act of turning off the light, she stayed her hand. Although she'd never been particularly afraid of the dark, Ravencrest had spooked her from the moment she'd driven up the access road. Feeling slightly paranoid, she kept the light on in the bathroom and left the door open a crack, so that a shaft of light slanted across the floor.

In the dim light she drifted toward the window and looked out. She'd approached the estate from the land side, where tall pines and probably redwoods had blocked her view. From this angle, she could see that the mansion was perched on the edge of a high cliff overlooking the sea. Moonlight gave her a view of waves rolling in, crashing against hidden obstructions and dark spires of rocks that poked up from the foam.

Far below she could hear the ebb and flow of the surf.

All at once the realization hit her that this was Troy's house. He had loved this place. Maybe he'd even stood at this very window looking down at the rocky coast. Until this moment she hadn't allowed herself to think much about what coming to his home would mean for her. But suddenly she felt close to him, closer than she had in years.

Seven years ago he'd told her about his home. He'd entranced her with his stories of exploring the cliffs and the sea caves that were accessible only at low tide and of his sailing expeditions into the wild waters offshore. She'd wanted to come here with him. She'd even secretly dreamed of living here—as his wife.

"Troy," she breathed, wishing that he was with her in this room. She remembered him so well, remembered how her first sight of him had taken her breath away. He'd walked into the parlor to greet her and Helen, and she'd found herself facing a tall, handsome man with tanned skin and wind-tossed hair that was just a beat too long. She'd taken him in in one swift draft, then focused on his eyes. They were vibrant hazel, fringed by dark lashes. And they'd turned warm when he'd looked at her.

"I'm Troy. And you must be Helen's friend Bonnie," he said.

"Yes. I've heard so much about you."

He smiled. "And I've heard about you. But I wasn't prepared for that charming Southern accent."

She'd blushed then, but he'd put her at ease immediately. Over the next few days they'd spent a lot of time together. Maybe too much time, as far as Helen was con-

cerned, because she'd complained that Troy was mo-
nopolizing her friend.

One of her most vivid memories was of dancing with
him, instinctively following the subtle signals of his body
as he'd led her around the front porch of the London
summer home.

Then there was the time he had come up behind her,
turned her in his arms and shocked her by lowering his
mouth to hers.

The thought made her skin tingle. Then she realized
that in fact she was shivering from the cool air.

Don't get all wound up with fantasies, she told herself.
Troy may not even be here. And if he is, he's not the
same man you knew all those years ago. And you're not
the same, either. Maybe he liked you better the way you
were. Or maybe not. Back then, she hadn't had the gump-
tion to reach out for what she wanted. She wasn't going
to repeat the same mistake again. Not if she could make
things come out the way she wanted them.

Pulling the drapes firmly across the window, she
quickly crossed to the bed and climbed between the
sheets, tugging the covers up to her chin. For a moment
she felt as though she had let Helen down. Almost everything that had happened since she'd arrived had been
out of her control. But she'd change that in the morning,
she vowed.

In a few minutes her own body heat began to warm
her and her mind began to drift. Soon sleep claimed her.

AS HE HAD SO OFTEN in the past few weeks, he stood on
the cliff. Dangerously close to the edge, yet he felt no
fear. Heights had never bothered him, and the sound of
breakers crashing against the shoreline had always

soothed him. Those were some of the things he remembered.

Mist swirled around him as he gazed down at the water pounding against the rocks fifty feet below. He had been drawn back to this spot, again and again. Below him was the stairway that led to the landing dock.

He had climbed that stairway a few weeks ago. He remembered that much. Then...

Suddenly it seemed important to grasp on to that memory, but it flitted away, as had so many of the thoughts that drifted through his mind like autumn leaves floating on a slow-running stream.

A man and a woman had come here. He remembered that.

They had told him... What?

Done what?

He didn't know. Perhaps he didn't want to know. Because on some hidden level, he sensed danger in the memory. It could hurt him badly. Like the blow on the head.

He remembered the pain and the blackness that had swallowed him up.

He shoved that memory aside, too. There was a strange kind of comfort in the blank space that took its place. A cold comfort. If he didn't know, perhaps it wasn't true.

And then there was the guilt. It was always with him. But it didn't choke off his breath now, because he couldn't remember what it was he had done. He just knew it was something very bad. He could feel it trying to sneak up on him and he clenched his eyes closed, willing it not to capture his mind.

As he'd prayed it would, the wisp of a memory flitted away. He stood very still, lifting his face to the wind, welcoming the chill.

Again, by force of will, he brought his attention to the present. To the newcomer, the woman who had arrived by car.

He had seen her, touched her shoulder. And for a little space of time, the tight, cold place inside his heart had loosened.

She had told them her name was Bree Brennan. Or was it Bonnie?

That sounded more familiar. Or maybe his memory was wrong.

His damn defective memory. Sometimes it was a curse and sometimes a blessing.

Another image worked its way into his mind. The child. Dinah. He had talked to her, drawn solace from her, given her comfort. At least he thought he had, though he couldn't bring any of their recent conversations into sharp focus. But he sensed a connection with her. A longing. A need to keep her safe and to protect her.

It was part of the guilt.

But that wasn't why he had gone to her room. Over and over. He needed to see her, to watch her sleep and to assure himself that she was still safe.

Quickly, he found his way down from the cliff, into the house, into the child's bedroom, where he stood beside her bed, gazing down at her.

She stirred in her sleep but didn't waken. He reached out a hand, then let it fall back to his side. Better not to disturb her now. He would let her be.

But the woman…

He would go to the woman. She had come back to him at last. The thought of her set off a humming in his head. An eagerness. An urgency. A need to recapture the past.

BREE'S EYES SNAPPED open.

Fear leaped inside her chest as she fought to remember

where she was. Then, from below her, she heard the crashing of waves against solid rock, and recent events flashed through her mind: the flight from Baltimore, the drive from San Francisco, Ravencrest and everyone she had encountered since arriving at this cold, massive house.

Her jaw clenched. She made an effort to relax and almost succeeded, until it registered that the room was dark, except for a small beam of moonlight filtering through a crack at the edge of the drapes.

But she'd deliberately left the light on in the bathroom. Why wasn't it burning now? Had the electricity gone off all over the house, or had someone turned off the light in her private quarters?

A tremor rippled across her skin as her gaze shot to the door that led to the hallway. It was closed.

Mentally, she went over her actions before going to bed. She'd been so tired she could barely function, but she did remember locking the door.

Under the covers, her nails dug into her palms as her hands clenched. Maybe that had awakened her—the small noise of the latch springing open. Or had someone come in another way?

Silently she damned herself for falling into bed without thinking things through. She should have checked the closet for hidden passages. And she should have fetched the gun from her suitcase.

It wasn't an ordinary gun. In today's climate she never would have risked trying to pack a regular handgun in her luggage. This was a special model designed by Randolph Security, a weapon that came apart into innocuous-looking pieces. She should have put it together, but she simply hadn't thought she'd need the gun in her locked bedroom.

Now she lay very still under the covers, her eyes slitted, trying to look as though she was still asleep. Her gaze flicked to the bathroom door, to the closet, probing the shadows, as she fought the feeling that the walls were pressing in around her.

She saw no one, heard no one, yet she sensed she was no longer alone in the room. The air around her seemed to have thickened so that it was difficult to take in a full breath. And she was sure that somebody or something was watching her.

Strangely, her body felt drugged, and she was afraid that if she tried to move an arm or a leg, it would be impossible to make the muscles work. All she could do was lie here, waiting for something to happen, her breath shallow.

Earlier, on the access road leading to the mansion, mist had slithered in white tendrils along the blacktop. Now, somehow, that same mist had crept into the bedroom, spreading across the floor like a white, undulating river of vapor.

The effect was eerie and so totally out of her experience that she could only stare at the foglike wisps while the edge of panic sank its sharp claws into her.

She knew a scream was locked in her throat. Yet at the same time, she felt a kind of humming anticipation. Something was going to happen. Was already happening.

A cloud drifted across the moon and the almost nonexistent light around her faded to black. A small gasp escaped her lips, a mere puff of air. If she could have made her muscles work, she would have sprung off the bed and dashed toward the door.

But her limbs were heavy, heavy as sandbags. At the

same time, a feverish expectation swelled inside her until she felt she would explode if something didn't happen.

Please. The supplication was only in her mind. She didn't have the power to speak out loud as she lay there with her heart thumping inside her chest. Slowly, inexorably, she sensed someone coming toward her. It was a man. She didn't hear his footsteps, but she detected his clean male scent mixed with the smell of soap and spicy aftershave. The scent she had caught outside on the driveway. Only more potent.

And suddenly her anticipation was stronger than her fear.

She knew he had come to a stop beside the bed, knew he was bending over her. In the depths of the darkness she couldn't see him, but she knew very well he was there. She should order him out of her bedroom. Yet the words stayed locked in her throat.

The air around her stirred and she felt his warm sweet breath against her face. For heartbeats, nothing more happened. Then she felt a gentle pressure against her lips.

It was a light kiss, butterfly light, brushing back and forth. A caress that teased and tantalized her senses even as it set off a shiver that was part sensual response and part fear.

For the moment at least, fear won, and she found her voice. "No."

He didn't accept the denial. Instead he absorbed the word of protest from her lips. Deliberately, he intensified the kiss, increased the breathless feeling in her chest as his lips moved over hers with practiced male assurance.

Her eyes drifted closed. Her heart stopped and then started again in overtime. She wanted to lift her arms. To push him away? To pull him close? She couldn't say which, and she did neither. She only lay there with her eyes closed, drawn into the experience until she was returning the kiss—tentatively at first and then with more passion as her need for him grew stronger.

For a long time their lips were the only point of contact. As he sensed her acceptance, his mouth opened, became more possessive. He was a skilled lover who knew what he was doing, knew how to surprise and tease. The kiss deepened, then became momentarily more shallow. His tongue played with the sensitive tissue at the insides of her lips, then probed into the corners.

When he caught her lower lip between his teeth and gently nipped at her, she heard a small moan escape her throat.

Her response seemed to please him. He touched her then, his fingers stroking her cheeks, her jawline, her neck, moving downward, sending tingles of sensation over her skin.

He slid his hands under the covers, his fingers skimming the warm skin of her shoulders, stopping to play with the straps of her gown, which brought another small moan from her.

She found her voice, enough voice for one word. "Troy?"

He didn't answer. She didn't even know if it was him. The only thing she knew was that this was neither of the other men she had met this evening. It couldn't be.

His lips left hers to flutter soft kisses over her closed eyelids, her brows, the tender line where her hair met her cheek. She felt his warm breath against her skin.

"Troy?" she asked again, her voice high and breathy as she responded to him.

Again he remained silent, never stopping the kisses and touches. His skin must have heated in response to her because the wonderful scent of his body had intensified.

She was enveloped in the sensual spell he was weaving. She wanted more from him.

As if he knew her desires, his hands slipped lower, playing with the edge of her gown where it rested against the tops of her breasts.

The kiss had started like a whisper of sensation against her lips. His touch was like that now. Light and playful. Teasing, even.

She responded with a flood of tingling warmth spreading downward through her body to the hollow place that had opened up inside her.

She could imagine her face, the dazed, drugged look. She no longer felt the bed beneath her body. Instead she seemed to float on the surface of a deep, warm pool of sensuality. But down in the far depths she felt doubt stirring. In some part of her mind she knew that this was wrong. It had to be wrong. Whether this man was Troy or not, he had come to her in the night without announcing his name or his intentions. He had come to her bed like a phantom lover.

The dark image was powerful in its dampening effect. The fear that had momentarily receded into the background leaped to the front of her mind again.

All at once, she felt as if she'd been under an evil, sensual spell. And through her own will, she had been released. Her eyes flew open. It was still dark in the room and she couldn't see the man who hovered over her. But her hands moved swiftly and surely as they came up to push him away.

For a millisecond she thought she felt the resistance of

his warm flesh, of muscle and bone. Then her hands pressed upward through chilled, empty air. He was gone. Vanished, as silently and as swiftly as he had come to her.

Chapter Three

For several heartbeats the room remained in the clutches of darkness. Then, perhaps in response to her urgent need, the clouds moved away from the moon and once again a sliver of radiance seeped through the crack at the edge of the drapes. In the cold, dim light that streamed across the room, Bree saw that she was alone.

Her midnight visitor had vanished—along with the mist that had rippled across the floor. Or had the mist just been the product of her overheated imagination?

Her heart was still pounding as she pushed herself up, pressed her back against the pillows and looked around the chamber.

"Troy?" she questioned, her voice no more than a breathy whisper. Once more there was no answer.

And no proof that the man who had come to her bed was Troy London, she thought, goose bumps blooming on her skin. In the darkness she hadn't seen him, only felt his touch and his scorching kiss as he'd woven his erotic spell around her.

Her skin heated at the memory. Her gaze flew to the door, but it was shut, the way she'd left it.

Now that she was alone, the whole experience seemed

cloaked in unreality. The mist, the man, her reaction that was so totally unlike her normal response.

Her visitor had come to her in the dead of night and coaxed a totally sensual response from her. Then, when she'd regained her senses, the rational part of her mind had been terrified.

At the same time, there was no way that she could deny the sexual pull toward her midnight caller. Raising her fingers, she touched them lightly to her lips, brushing them back and forth, feeling a small tingling afterburn of the sensations he'd generated.

Oh, yes, she remembered his touch. But she remembered other sensations, too. She'd felt strange, drugged, compelled, as if she'd been under some kind of evil magic spell.

Even as thoughts of black magic formed, her mind rejected the explanation—and jumped to a more acceptable alternative. Maybe the whole experience had simply been a dream, a very vivid dream brought on by her exhaustion and her own sexual needs. She'd been thinking about Troy, remembering him just before she'd gone to bed. And she'd been hoping to encounter him. So it made sense that she had conjured him up in the dark of the night. And conjured up the sensuality, too, if she were honest.

Because she'd never given up her secret dream of getting back together with Troy, and she'd never stopped wanting him.

She'd been a virgin seven years ago when she'd first met him, and she was pretty sure he'd known it. He'd been careful of her, going slowly, awakening her sensuality with touches and kisses that had become more intimate over time. She remembered that first thrilling moment when he'd cupped her breast then played with her beaded nipple through the fabric of her blouse and bra.

They'd been dancing on the porch then, their bodies swaying in slow, provocative rhythm. When he'd slid his hands down her body and pulled her against his arousal, her own need had leaped to meet his.

She'd been exhilarated with the knowledge that they'd been on the verge of making love. Then her mother had gotten sick and she'd gone rushing back to North Carolina. Mom's health was fragile, and she couldn't be left alone, so they'd moved to Baltimore, where Aunt Martha could take care of her while Bree was in school.

She'd lost track of Troy in the flurry of activity surrounding the move. Later, she'd told herself it was for the best. Still, she'd been shocked and hurt when she'd heard that he'd gotten married so soon after she'd left.

Then, because he'd taken a wife, she'd told herself it was wrong to still want him. And mostly she'd managed to keep him out of her thoughts. But Helen's call had changed everything.

Maybe the real reason, the secret reason, she'd come rushing to Ravencrest was that she wanted to take up where they'd left off.

Unbidden, more scenes came winging back to her from the summer of her sophomore year in college—when she'd been head over heels in love with Troy. It wasn't just sex. The two of them had seemed so right for each other. They'd gotten into long discussions about all sorts of topics from world politics to the running of the family cattle ranch. They'd gone for rides in the mountains, carried along a picnic lunch so they wouldn't have to come back for hours. He'd taken her to the barn where she'd been entranced by a newborn foal.

She'd thought their relationship was heading somewhere important. And then it had all been snatched away from her.

As those memories from the past flooded through her mind and body, it was impossible to stay in the bed where he'd come to her. Throwing aside the covers, she swung her legs over the edge, thumping her feet onto the floor as she looked around.

Weaving slightly, she crossed the room. First she tried the door, just to make sure. It was locked—the way she'd left it.

With a sigh, she backtracked to the window. When she opened the curtains and pushed at the bottom sash, it slid upward with only minimal resistance.

The cold outside air sent a shiver rippling over her skin, but she didn't step back. Cautiously, she stuck her head out and took in the scene. The stars and moon gleamed in a black velvet sky. A path of moonlight wavered on the dark surface of the restless ocean below her.

Dragging her gaze away from the mesmerizing sky and the water, she inspected the wall of the building. It rose above her for two more floors like a man-made extension of the cliff. And like the cliff, there were rough stones that an agile climber might be able to use for hand- and footholds. But could anyone climbing the wall have gotten away so quickly?

Maybe, if he'd slipped inside another room. Or if he was a mountain climber, like Troy. That summer, she'd watched with her heart in her throat as he'd scaled sheer cliffs. There was no reason he couldn't do the same thing now.

Suddenly feeling dizzy, she pulled her head back inside, then shut the window and sprung the latch.

Her next stop was the bathroom, where she felt around for the light switch. It was in the off position, and the light came on as soon as she flipped it up. Blinking in the yellow glow, she waited for several seconds then checked her watch. It was one in the morning. She'd gone to bed around seven, so she'd slept almost six hours. That meant she probably wasn't going back to sleep anytime soon.

With a small shrug, she crossed to the sink, scooped up some water in her hands and took several sips. The tingling cold helped ground her. Deliberately, she brought up more details from the disturbing encounter, examining the facts and her feelings.

Either she'd dreamed up the whole thing or a man had come to her room, a man whose presence had frightened her but whose seductive touch had captivated her. He hadn't been rough with her. On the contrary, his attention had been gentle yet thrilling. Still, she'd known he shouldn't be there and when she'd reached to push him away, her hands had contacted only empty air.

Once more, her skin prickled. She wanted to cling to the dream theory, but she knew that would be dangerous.

Just as it was dangerous to get all wound up with memories of Troy—or to mix them up with the present.

She squeezed her eyes closed, trying to talk herself out of the feeling of intensity he'd created within her. Intensity she'd seldom experienced in her lifetime.

Of course she'd had relationships with other men since her almost affair with Troy. In fact, she'd done her best to forget Troy London and to get serious about someone else. But none of her other boyfriends had seemed like the soul mate she'd wanted for a marriage partner. And she'd known deep down that she was comparing each of them unfavorably to Troy.

She snorted. Talk about carrying a torch! Obviously the man had gotten over her. He'd married not long after that sweet summer encounter. And Helen had said that his wife's death had devastated him.

Yet tonight he hadn't come to her like a man still pining for his lost wife. He'd come to her like a lover. And now she struggled to figure out what that encounter meant.

Again she touched her lips, remembering the kisses in the darkness. She was making assumptions about his identity. Could she be sure he was the same man who had held her in his arms seven years ago?

She couldn't answer that question. Maybe if she'd seen him tonight she would know for sure. But she was forced to rely on her other senses—on the memory of his long-ago kisses and caresses. She'd been a lot younger then. So had Troy. His kisses had been different, less skillful back then. But she could put that down to his lack of maturity and experience. And her own immaturity, too.

Resolutely she reentered the bedroom and switched on the overhead light. Then she turned to the closet. The door was closed, and she hesitated for heartbeats as she stared at the dark wood as if trying to penetrate it with her gaze.

If he was inside, she should clear out. Yet he hadn't hurt her. He hadn't demanded anything. He'd only taken as much as she'd wanted to give. And he probably wasn't anywhere around now.

She recognized all those thoughts as rationalization. Still, before she could stop herself, she grasped the knob, turned it and pulled the door open. The closet was empty—and as dark as she remembered.

She breathed out a small sigh, then kneeled on the floor, felt around in her suitcase and found the flashlight that she'd brought along for emergencies. When her heart rate had calmed a little, she began investigating the closet, shining the light along the walls, over the ceiling and down to the floor, which was made of the same wood boards as in the bedroom. The walls and ceiling were old-fashioned plaster, except for the back of the closet, which was wood paneling. Holding the light in one hand, she shone the beam over the surface. With the other hand, she ran her fingers and palm lightly over the wood, taking care not to pick up any stray splinters in the process. She thought she detected a line where two pieces of paneling came together—which proved nothing more than that the surface had been applied in sections.

Making her hand into a fist, she rapped her knuckles lightly against the wood, first on one side, then on the other, and finally in the middle. The sound seemed different—more solid in the middle and on the right side, more hollow on the left.

Unsure of how to proceed, she tried pressing on various parts of the panel, disappointed when nothing happened. Exasperated, she put down her flashlight and pressed with two hands, trying different random patterns. When she pushed with one hand near the top of the panel and the other near the middle, there was a soft click. In the next second the wall swung inward, revealing a dark, yawning cavern.

She stared into the blackness, automatically wishing the door hadn't opened. Then, firming her jaw, she picked up the flashlight again and shone it into the opening. A long, dark passage stretched in front of her. The old Bonnie Brennan would probably have shut the door again, gone back to bed and pulled the covers over her head. The old Bonnie Brennan had been passive and timid. The new Bree Brennan knew she had to find out where the passage led because there was no safety in her room as long as someone could sneak in at will.

But the new Bree Brennan was no fool. She wasn't going to do it dressed in her nightgown. And she wasn't going to act like the dumb heroine of a Gothic novel. She was going to get her gun.

Digging through her suitcase, she began to pull out the separate parts of the weapon. The barrel was a narrow flashlight. The clip was a waterproof box filled with ''medicine capsules.'' The stock was a soap dish.

After finding all the components, she sat on the bed and put the gun together.

Carefully she tested her construction skills, then loaded in a clip and got comfortable again with the feel of the weapon in her hand. Before she'd left Baltimore, she'd trained with this pistol on a firing range until she'd felt confident that it would protect her if she needed it.

Turning back to her suitcase, she found a T-shirt and a pair of sweatpants. After pulling them on, she got out socks and running shoes. When she was better outfitted for exploring, she picked up her gun and the flashlight and faced the tunnel again.

As she played the beam over the walls, she saw that they were made of the same paneling as the back of the closet. The floor, however, was stone.

Spiderwebs blurred the line where the ceiling met the walls, and she braced for musty air. But it had an unexpected freshness, as though there were some access to the outside. When she licked her finger and held it up, she detected a faint breeze.

Some part of her thought it might not be a dumb idea to turn around and go back. At the same time another part of her wondered if she was being compelled to sneak down this tunnel by some outside force. The same force that had held her captive in bed when she'd first awakened.

Just to prove she could, she stopped in her tracks and thought about what she was doing. It made sense that the man who'd come to her room was long gone. But if he'd gotten into her bedroom through this tunnel, she wanted to know what lay at the other end.

"Troy?" she called.

He didn't answer, and she hadn't expected him to. Still, calling out to him made her pulse beat faster.

Gun in one hand and flashlight in the other, she moved along the passage, feeling the floor slope slightly downward as she went. She stayed close to the right-hand wall, and about ten feet into the tunnel, the surface changed from paneling to stone.

After about twenty paces, the tunnel curved to the right, abruptly turning a corner so that when she swiveled back, she could no longer see the closet where she'd entered.

If she turned off the flashlight, she knew she would be in total darkness. A jolt of claustrophobia grabbed her by the throat and she had to pause and press her arm against the rough stone. Closing her eyes, she took several deep, steadying breaths. When she felt more in control, she started moving forward again, still counting the paces.

She had taken perhaps ten more steps when disaster struck, overtaking her so suddenly that she had no preparation. One moment she was standing on solid ground, the next, the floor of the tunnel fell out from under her feet.

A scream tore from her throat as she dropped the flashlight and the gun, clawing at the wall with both hands. But there was no way she could stop herself from tumbling into space like a rag doll tossed over the edge of a cliff.

The gun clattered to the stone floor. The flashlight

plummeted farther downward, the glass smashing and the light going dark as it hit something solid far below her.

The world seemed to slow, so that she felt trapped in a bubble. She had time to think, time to consider her fate. She would follow the flashlight down, her mind screamed as she braced for the impact of her body striking rock far below.

But it never happened. A man's strong arms caught her, stopping her downward plunge in midfall. For a heart-stopping moment it felt as if she were standing on nothing but air, her legs dangling helplessly as he held her upper body in his grasp.

Rocks continued to tumble over the precipice into some black, bottomless pit, the impact reverberating in the confined space.

Her breath came hard and fast as she clung to him. Pressing her face against his chest, she struggled to make sense of what had happened.

Just as in the bedroom, she couldn't see him in the darkness, only feel the solid shape of his body and the soft fabric of his flannel shirt as he folded her close.

It was him, the man who had come to her bed, she thought, leaning into his strength as the scent of soap and spice enveloped her.

In the darkness, she let him drag her a few steps back, away from the place where the floor had dropped out from under her feet. For long moments she was happy to simply nestle in his arms, eyes closed.

"Thank you," she murmured. "Thank you for being there when I needed you."

She felt his head nod, his chin brushing the top of her hair, felt his large hands slide possessively up and down her back, stroking, soothing, keeping her close in the circle of his arms. Clasping her more tightly, he turned his head so that he could press his lips against her hair, while his hands trailed over her back, along her spine.

It was tempting to simply drift, wrapped in his comfort and care. But finally she roused herself. "Tell me who you are," she said.

As before, he didn't speak.

She had been feeling calm and protected, but suddenly a flare of anger overtook her.

"Are you Troy? Answer me, damn you! What kind of games are you playing with me?" As she spoke, she angled her head up, trying to see him in the blackness. But she was just as frustrated as she had been in the bedroom. Without the flashlight, the tunnel was like the inside of a whale's belly.

He took advantage of her upturned face and open lips. Instead of speaking, he brought his mouth down on hers in a kiss that took her by surprise.

There was a charged moment when she tried to tell him what she thought of his evasive maneuvers. But he didn't give her the opportunity. Instead he took her by storm, his lips demanding, insisting, commanding as his hands clamped over her shoulders, holding her to him.

She might have tried to pull away, except that below the surface of his assault, she sensed a need that tugged at her with a desperation that made her heart turn over.

Without giving herself time to consider the wisdom of her actions, she allowed her lips to soften against his. It was only the barest signal of surrender, but he reacted immediately.

The kiss changed from a ravishment to a meeting of two equal forces. On a sigh, she gave herself over to it, experimenting with the sensations he was generating within her, rubbing her mouth back and forth against his, then taking his lower lip between her teeth the way he'd done in the bedroom, staking a claim on his flesh.

It was then that she heard a deep, throaty sound well in him. The sound was the first he had made since he'd come to her in the bedroom, one part of her mind realized. That thought fled as he took back dominance of the kiss, angling his head, moving his lips against hers, sipping from her, inciting her, then soothing with masterful control.

She heard wind roaring in her ears, a cyclone brewing. Somehow he was the only safe refuge. She felt fire sweep her up, fire that came from him and kindled a roar of heat in her belly.

The kiss tasted of dark needs and the wild heather clinging to the cliffs.

When he silently asked her to open her mouth, she did his bidding, then shivered as his tongue swept along the sensitive tissue of her lips.

She felt his hunger, felt her own hunger leap up to match his. He pressed her back so that she was trapped between the rock wall and the solid barrier of his body.

The cold stone might have chilled her if the heat of his body hadn't seeped into her flesh and bone. It was like being caught in the blast from an open furnace. And she might burn to a cinder if she wasn't careful. That thought brought back a measure of sanity.

It took a tremendous act of will, but she managed to raise her hands, pushing gently against his chest. "Don't. We have to talk. You were in my room. Then you came here—and saved me from that pit."

In the dark, the air stirred, and she thought he had nodded again. But he didn't volunteer any words of agreement.

The silence made her boil with frustration and she

grabbed his shoulders and shook him. "Dammit, I don't even know if you're Troy! I think you must be Troy. But it's been so long." The wistful sound of her own voice made her stop and drag in a calming breath. Slowly, deliberately, she let it ease out again. "Every time I try to have a conversation with you, you kiss me. What's wrong with you? Have you lost the ability to talk?"

Her heart thumped in her chest as she waited for an answer, half afraid that it was actually true—that somehow he'd been struck mute.

"I can speak to you," he said, sounding surprised and relieved, as though he'd just discovered that he possessed the ability.

"Thank God!" she breathed. "Helen is worried about you. She said she got e-mails from you that sounded strange."

"She got e-mails from me?"

"Yes!" Her hands tightened on his arms. "Troy, what happened to you? What's wrong?"

He didn't answer the question. Instead he said very clearly and distinctly, "I didn't send her any e-mails. She's lying."

Chapter Four

"Helen is lying? About what?" she demanded, her fingers digging into the tense muscles of Troy's arms. If it was Troy. She didn't even know the answer to that question yet. Not for sure.

He shifted his weight from one foot to the other, as though the topic made him uncomfortable.

"Please. You can't just come out with a statement like that. You have to tell me what you mean."

When he remained silent, she struggled to contain her frustration and she heard the strident note in her own voice when she said, "Helen sent me to find out what's wrong at Ravencrest. What's wrong with *you!*"

"She sent you?" he asked, surprise gathering in his voice.

"Yes."

"Helen wouldn't do that. She…" He didn't finish the sentence, simply let it trail off, as though he had forgotten what he intended to say. Or thought better of giving any more away.

She had gone beyond frustration to simmering anger. "Troy, I was sleeping in my bed when you came waltzing into my room in the middle of the night and started kissing me. You can't do that, then act like we have nothing to talk about.''

"Why not?" he asked slowly, as though social conventions were a deep mystery.

She needed to see the expression on his face. Was he having fun with her? But the darkness made it impossible to judge his intent.

When the silence stretched, she got back to basics. "Are you Troy London?" she asked.

"I...don't know."

The answer and the tentative way he spoke were so unexpected that it sent a sizzle along her nerve endings. "What do you mean, you don't know? How can you not know who you are?"

"Do you want me to lie?"

"Certainly not."

It sounded as if he was claiming he had amnesia. She didn't know much about the condition, but she remembered when a friend's mother had had no memory of a bad car accident.

She sighed. "Do you remember what happened to you? I mean, do you know why you've lost your memory?"

"No," he murmured, sounding so lost and alone that her heart squeezed.

In the darkness she reached for his hand. Without speaking, she folded her slender fingers around his larger ones. Almost at once he shifted his grip so that he was holding on to her, the pressure increasing as they stood in the blackness of the tunnel.

She remembered him as strong and vital. A man of action. A man without fear. She remembered the time they'd been walking on the ranch and a rattlesnake had slithered out from behind a rock and he'd beaten it to death with a stick while she'd gasped at him to be careful. There were other memories that were just as strong. Tender memories. Like the way he'd gathered a bouquet of wildflowers from the hills around the ranch and set them in a pretty blue-and-white pitcher in her room. He'd been tough and masculine, yet he hadn't been afraid to show her his sensitive side.

Now…

Now it was hard to believe this was the same man.

Of course, he could be putting on an elaborate charade, although she didn't think so. Something was badly wrong, but she couldn't say what. Not without more information, which he wouldn't or couldn't give her.

Her mind spun with questions. Had he fallen from the cliffs? Had a stroke? Or had he been drugged?

And then there was his preference for the darkness. Why wouldn't he let her see him? Fear shot through her as a ready explanation leaped into her mind. He *had* been in an accident—and his face was scarred, which was why he was staying hidden.

She reached up with her free hand to touch him, and he stepped quickly back as though he could see perfectly well in the dark and knew what she was thinking. The sudden withdrawal gave credence to her speculation.

"You were hurt," she said.

"Yes."

"It's all right. I mean, if you don't like the way you look, it's not going to…offend me. Is that it? Is that what's wrong?"

"Stop trying to come up with explanations," he said with more force than he'd exhibited thus far in all their interactions. "You're not doing either one of us any good."

She might have protested. Instead she gave him the

space he was demanding. He had come to her. That was a start. "All right," she said simply.

In the darkness she heard him suck in a deep, sighing breath and then let it out in a rush. Again he reached for her, but this time his hand only rested lightly on her arm. "You should leave this place. If you stay here you're going to get into trouble."

Her reaction was swift and sharp. "I came here to find out what happened to you—and to make sure Dinah is all right. Don't you care about her?"

The hand on her arm clenched then opened. "Dinah," he said softly. "I forgot about Dinah."

"How could you forget about your own daughter?"

"Is she?"

Lord, what was that supposed to mean? Was he saying the child wasn't his, or that he wasn't Troy London?

She dragged a hand through her hair, sweeping it back from her face. Suddenly she felt as if she were an actor who'd been shoved onstage in a play for which she'd missed the rehearsals and lost the script. Now she was in the middle of the action and she had no idea what was expected of her. And in the back of her mind, she couldn't let go of the feeling that Helen London had orchestrated the whole thing.

She canceled that thought as unfair. Helen had warned her that something bad was going on at Ravencrest. It was Bree's job to figure out what it was.

Still, the whole situation was overwhelming. She certainly couldn't answer Troy's question about Dinah. She didn't know how to deal with him. Yet she couldn't simply turn around and go back to her room. Not now.

"Do you know who I am?" she finally asked.

This time he answered more quickly. "I heard you say you were Bonnie Brennan. Bree. I like that better."

"You were listening when I arrived?"

"I listen in on what's happening here." He stroked his hand up and down her arm. "You were talking to Nola."

"Yes."

So he'd been hiding, eavesdropping on her conversation in the hall. She wasn't going to press him on that. Instead, now that they were communicating a little better, she went back to his earlier bombshell. "Why did you say Helen was lying?"

"Because she…wouldn't call anyone for help. She's too independent."

That was a good description of Helen—under ordinary circumstances. But not in this case. Bree sighed. "She's stuck halfway around the world and she's worried about you. So you're wrong."

"You're Helen's friend," he said, sounding as if he wasn't quite sure.

"Yes, I'm her friend from college. I was Bonnie Brennan back then. I changed my name to Bree."

"Why?"

"I didn't like the woman I realized I was," she answered, unwilling to give any more away even as she fought off disappointment.

Didn't he remember her from the summer of her sophomore year, when they had been so close? At least she'd thought they were. It had been the most memorable time of her life, the most compelling relationship in her entire existence. It hurt to think that it had meant far less to him. Yet tonight there had been a breathtaking intensity between them. That must mean something, surely. Maybe even though he didn't remember her on a conscious level, he'd been drawn back to her.

He interrupted her thoughts with another pronouncement. "It's dangerous here. You have to go back."

"Back to Maryland?"

"Back to your room."

The firm, decisive delivery chilled her. He'd been holding her hand. He broke the contact, stepping away from her, leaving her standing in the dark.

"Troy!"

"Stay there. Don't move." His voice was sharp, commanding, urgent, and she froze.

One of his hands clamped on her shoulder, leading her around a sharp corner. "Look!"

In the next moment fire flared only a few yards in front of her face, the sudden light so unexpected after the total darkness that she couldn't focus. Dimly she saw a burning faggot of straw or sticks fly through the air, arching upward before it began to fall—not at her feet, but far, far below.

With a shock of amazement she realized she'd been so caught up in the conversation with Troy that she'd forgotten about the gaping pit.

The brand crashed onto the rocks, sending sparks flaring upward toward her.

She blinked, probing the darkness—and knew that in the moments when she'd been blinded, he'd slipped away.

"Troy?"

He didn't answer and she felt a shiver slither over her skin. He'd mesmerized her, made her forget about the dangerous drop-off.

Then, when he'd thrown the burning brand, she hadn't even seen him at all. She was still grappling with that when his voice drifted toward her, this time from far away.

"Go back," he said again. And then he was gone.

"Troy," she called, knowing even as she said his

name that she was absolutely alone. "Troy," she said again, despairingly, softly. "Don't run away from me. Let me help you."

Even as she called out to him, she knew he wasn't going to answer. He had left her here, left her with light. And she knew she should use the opportunity to go back down the tunnel.

But she could also see that there was a short path that led along the rim of the pit and around a corner to some other section of the underground passage—a section that was hidden from view.

He'd slipped away. He hadn't brushed past her. So the only way he could have gone was in the other direction.

The old Bonnie Brennan whispered that she would be a fool to follow him. He obviously knew his way around here, and she didn't. The new persona she'd worked so hard to create shouted that she had no other options.

It was clear Troy had sought her out because he was in trouble. Yet, at the same time, he didn't want to—or couldn't—give her any information.

What if he'd changed his mind about trusting her and this was her only chance to get some answers from him?

For a long moment she stood with her lower lip between her teeth, torn between safety and urgency. Yet deep down she silently acknowledged that one reason she'd come here was to test herself. To find out if she'd really changed from the timid woman of the past. To prove she wasn't her old wimpy self, she took a step forward and then another, hugging the rock wall, staying as far as she could from the pit. Although it was only six or eight feet to the other side, the journey seemed endless. She breathed a little sigh as she came out onto a wider space again.

But she could take only half a dozen steps forward

before she came up against a rockfall that totally blocked her forward progress.

"Troy?" she called out once more, hoping against hope that he would answer. He remained silent.

It seemed impossible for him to have gotten past that pile of loose boulders. So was he here somewhere, hiding?

As she stared at the dead-end tunnel, she saw the light from below flicker and she knew that the brand in the chasm wasn't going to burn much longer. If it went out while she was still over here, getting back along the narrow path would be all the more dangerous.

Quickly she retraced her steps, surprised that the light flared more brightly as she crossed the rocky passage. In her imagination, she couldn't help picturing Troy down there, holding up the torch for her. Was that where he'd gone? Down some flight of steps she couldn't see?

She had just stepped back onto the other side when the flame blazed up, then suddenly choked out.

In reaction, she felt her throat close and pressed her hand against the rock. After taking a moment to get her bearings, she eased around the corner and started back up the tunnel, keeping one hand on the rock.

At first she moved slowly down the passageway. But she picked up speed as she put distance between herself and the chasm, until she was almost running when she felt the surface under her feet change.

She was back in the part of the tunnel that led directly to her bedroom closet, and as she peered ahead of her, she saw the bedroom light that she'd left burning.

Relief surged through her as she stepped back into the closet. When her gaze flicked to the window, she saw gray morning light filtering around the edges of the curtain.

Turning on all the lights, she threw the closet door wide and made sure she understood how to operate the hidden entrance to the tunnel. Then she closed off the passage and stepped back into the bedroom. To her relief, she found a lock on the closet door.

Her lips set in a firm line, she transferred her suitcase to a shelf in the large bathroom and hung her few good clothes on the hook on the back of the door. Then she locked the closet, intending to keep it locked for the rest of her stay here.

She supposed someone could still come into the bedroom through the tunnel—if they wanted to break down the door. But they could also break down the entrance to the hall, for that matter. She glanced at the door, feeling suddenly as if someone were on the other side, listening to her every move.

Her jaw clenched and she thought about marching across the room and flinging the door open.

But she'd already had two confrontations this morning. And she was pretty sure she couldn't handle another one.

MOMENTS BEFORE Bree stepped back into the room, a hand quietly twisted the knob on the hall side of the bedroom door—and found it locked.

Now the person in the hall stood listening to the sound of footsteps moving quickly around inside the bedroom. What the hell was she so busy doing in there anyway?

She'd arrived looking worn out, and for a long time there had been no signs of life inside the room. Now she was definitely awake. Was she an early riser, or was it the time change from the east coast?

Either way, clearing out would be a good idea—in case she opened the door and discovered that someone was interested in what she was doing so early in the morning.

The watcher hurried away down the darkened hallway, thinking that if Ms. Brennan had been smart, she would have turned away before she'd driven through the gate. But now she was here. Locked in. Helpless to do anything but play the role that had been assigned to her.

AFTER DONNING a light blue sweater and jeans, Bree stood staring at the closet door.

She'd dropped her gun in the tunnel. And leaving it there could be a bad mistake, assuming someone besides Troy really could get into the passageway from the other end.

But she'd also dropped her flashlight—into the pit, if she wasn't mistaken. Despite her new resolve, the idea of going back there in the darkness made goose bumps rise on her skin. Besides, what chance did she have of finding the gun without a light?

With a sigh, she stepped to the window and looked out, studying the spellbinding panorama in the light of day.

Long ago Troy had described the house and the seascape. He'd painted a vivid word picture, but now she knew it was impossible to capture the rugged setting in words.

He'd told her he loved this place, that he was always drawn back here after his summers in the mountains. It did have a wild beauty—but a beauty that was as dangerous as it was picturesque. Perhaps that was part of the appeal for him, she thought as she watched the relentless power of the waves, particularly one spot where fierce currents pulled the ocean into a circular whirlpool of what must be icy-cold water.

As she stared at the awesome natural scene, her thoughts circled like the whirlpool back to the man who had come to her room last night. She was pretty sure he was Troy London. Definitely sure he was in some kind of trouble. And either he was pretending to have lost his memory or he was using memory loss as an excuse not to communicate.

About the present? Or about the past?

She snorted. The past was over for both of them. She was nothing like that naive girl who had traveled to Montana to visit a college friend. She'd taught school, buried her mother, found a job she loved with the Light Street Detective Agency, changed her life for the better. And he was different, too. He'd gotten married, had a daughter, buried a wife. But what if everything that had happened since that summer was less important than what was happening now?

Suppose he'd really lost his memory? Was he reaching out to her on some unconscious level because they'd shared an intense couple of weeks together one summer?

Of course, there was another explanation, just as plausible. He was cold-bloodedly using her—acting as though he wanted to make love because he knew that she'd been attracted to him and he thought he could get what he wanted from her.

Which was what exactly?

Was he up to something shady? Something illegal? Did he figure she was going to help him pull off some scheme he'd kept hidden from everyone? Even his sister. Maybe the Sterlings were even in on it and Helen simply didn't know about it.

Bree sighed as her mind spiraled back to the inconvenient fact that she still couldn't be absolutely sure the man who had kissed her so passionately last night was Troy London. What's more, no matter who he was, as far as she could tell, he'd vanished into thin air at the end of the tunnel.

Either she'd have to wait until he chose to contact her again or she'd have to find out where he was hiding. In some secret room in the house, a cave carved out of the rock, a hut on the grounds? She had no idea.

But she had a map of the house that Helen had given her. Now that she was actually here, she should be able to find Troy's bedroom and poke around.

But all of that would have to wait until later.

Quickly she put on a little makeup, then stood beside her door, listening intently before turning the lock. She told herself that she was being paranoid. There was no one on the other side. Still, as she stepped into the hall, she looked quickly left and right, letting out the breath she was holding when she saw the corridor was clear.

As she came to the place where Graves had disappeared, she stopped. Another man pulling a vanishing act! Last night she'd wanted to figure out where he'd gone. It must have been into another secret passage, and now she was wondering if that passage connected with the tunnel that opened into her closet.

There were curtains near the spot where he'd been standing. When she looked behind them, she found a wall covered with paneling, like the back of her closet.

Stepping partially behind the curtain, she knelt and began to examine the wall for signs of a hidden door.

She had just raised her right hand to tap on the paneling when the sound of footsteps coming down the hall made her freeze.

Chapter Five

"Do you mind telling me what you're doing?" a sharp voice asked. A voice Bree recognized.

Straightening, she slowly withdrew from behind the curtain to find herself facing Nola Sterling.

She had given herself a few seconds to think of an answer to the question. Going back to her Southern belle persona, she batted her eyes, looking confused.

"Oh, I swear, I'm so disorganized. It must be the jet lag and the long drive up here from the city. Last night I lost an earring. I was trying to find it."

Nola cocked her head, studying her with narrowed eyes. "But you're wearing earrings," she pointed out.

"Yes. I put in a different pair," Bree answered quickly.

Nola waited a beat, letting her squirm, before asking, "Any luck finding the missing one?"

"No. But I might have lost it somewhere else in the hall or even in my room." On a breath she continued, "It was shaped like a little rose. Really, it's such a pretty piece. And it belonged to my grandmother. I'd be simply devastated if it didn't turn up. Will you keep an eye out for it?" she asked, babbling on as though she were thrown off her stride. She was, of course. But not because of a piece of jewelry.

Under Nola's piercing gaze, she shifted from foot to foot.

"Of course," her hostess finally said. "But right now, you might want to come to breakfast, since you didn't have any dinner last night."

Bree cleared her throat. "How do you know that?"

"Mrs. Martindale mentioned it."

"Oh, right."

"Let me show you the way to the dining room."

As Nola started along the hall again, Bree walked several steps behind, because there wasn't room to walk abreast. Did Nola know that there were secret passages in the old house? If not, it was probably a good idea to keep her in the dark about the secrets of Ravencrest.

"I'm sure you were wondering why Mr. London didn't meet you yesterday," Nola said, glancing briefly over her shoulder, then lowered her voice so that Bree had to strain to hear her. "I'm afraid he's not well."

She felt a tremor flicker over her skin. "What's wrong with him? Is it something serious?" she managed to ask.

Nola lowered her voice another notch, so that Bree had to step closer. "He's had a nervous breakdown."

Her rejoinder was instantaneous. "That's hard to believe."

"Why?"

"I guess it was an automatic reaction," she said lamely. "When Ms. London hired me, she didn't say anything about her brother's mental condition," she added, thinking as she said the words that they weren't exactly true. Actually, Helen *had* discussed Troy's mental condition. She'd been worried about him since the death of his wife. She'd said he was depressed and not acting like himself. So could he have suddenly gotten worse? Could he somehow have gone over the edge? Was *that* the real answer to her questions about him?

Her mouth had gone dry and she swallowed to speak. "Where is he?" she asked.

"He exhibited some violent tendencies, so he's confined to his room."

"Confined? You mean locked in? Is that necessary?"

"I don't know. His doctor thought it was better for him to stay in a stress-free environment after he smashed one of the antique clocks downstairs," Nola answered smoothly, her expression hidden from Bree.

Bree struggled to take in that information.

"Who is his doctor?"

"Dr. John Smith."

Bree struggled not to snort out a laugh. John Smith. How convenient. "He's local?" she asked carefully. "Would it be possible for me to speak to him?"

"I believe he's from San Francisco. Not that that's any of your business. You were hired to teach his daughter, not concern yourself with his mental health."

"His condition *is* my concern if it affects my work here. Or if it affects his daughter."

Nola answered swiftly and succinctly. "If you're worried about the working conditions at Ravencrest, you can always leave."

"Um, yes…" Bree dragged in a breath and let it out. "Thanks for your insights," she murmured, carefully considering the conversation. Either Nola was flat-out lying to her about Troy being locked in his room, or she was unaware that he was roaming the estate at night. If the man Bree had talked to *was* Troy.

Then there was the question of Nola's motives. Was

she really concerned about Troy's health, or was she simply covering up his disappearance?

They had reached the stairs. Bree followed the other woman down, then through the entrance hall and into the back of the house.

The gold-and-blue dining room was on the cliff side of the house, with huge windows that provided a spectacular view of the restless ocean. Bree stood transfixed, struck once more by the wild, isolated setting and the waves pounding against the rocks.

Nola watched her for a moment. "You never get used to it," she said.

"Does it frighten you?" Bree asked.

"Why should it?"

"I guess because it's a reminder of the power of nature."

"I don't waste my time being frightened of nature," the woman snapped, then turned her back on the window and marched toward a sideboard covered with a white cloth.

Bree saw that various dishes had been set out. At one end was cold cereal, milk and cartons of fruit yogurt. At the other end were several chafing dishes with scrambled eggs, bacon and hash browns.

Bree hadn't eaten since the afternoon before, but just looking at the heavy, hot food made her stomach roil. Instead she opted for cereal and peach yogurt.

Her hostess had already made a similar selection, and they carried their choices to the long dining room table. Following the other woman's lead, Bree also poured herself a cup of tea from the cart against the wall.

As she and Nola were seating themselves, a door at the far end of the room opened and a short, plump woman bustled in.

She was wearing a crisp white apron over a flowered dress. And her salt-and-pepper hair was pulled back in a bun.

''Well,'' she said, ''I see you've gotten settled all right. I'm Mrs. Martindale. We spoke over the intercom last night. I've baked some nice lemon and poppy seed muffins for breakfast this morning.'' She thrust forward a small basket, emitting a delicious aroma.

''Thank you. That's very kind.'' Bree took one and transferred it to her plate before the woman set the basket down.

During the short exchange, Nola Sterling mechanically spooned up milk and cereal as though she couldn't wait for the housekeeper to leave.

Bree's suspicion was confirmed several moments after the door had closed again.

''That woman takes liberties,'' Nola muttered.

''Oh?''

''She's supposed to be a servant but she acts like she's the grand dame of this place.''

''Um,'' Bree answered. She had very little experience with servants, but she'd thought that Mrs. Martindale was simply being friendly—in a rather old-fashioned sort of way.

Nola leaned back in her chair. Cradling her teacup in her hands, she said, ''I hope you slept all right last night.''

Was her hostess finally relaxing and making an attempt at polite conversation? Bree wondered. Or was she fishing for evidence that the new teacher was going to crack under the strain of living at Ravencrest?

''Fine,'' she answered, vividly aware that her bland statement was a lie.

Nola continued to study her, letting the moment stretch

until Bree wanted to squirm in her seat. But she managed to keep still. Deliberately, she picked up her own cup and took a sip, looking down into the honey-colored liquid.

"So you weren't…bothered by the resident ghost?" Nola pressed, watching Bree carefully.

She knew the words had been chosen for their dramatic content. Still, her head jerked up.

In danger of spilling the tea, she set down her cup abruptly, so that it clattered into the saucer, the sound ringing through the dining room. "What ghost?" she asked, her voice coming out high and thin.

Nola gave her a satisfied smile that grated on Bree's nerves. "Are you afraid of ghosts, Bree?"

"I've never encountered one."

"Well, I'm sure you will. If you haven't already. The mansion is supposed to be haunted. By several ghosts, actually. The most, uh, bothersome one is the ghost of a man whose wife fell over the edge of the cliff one night in a storm. She was killed, and he never got over her death. When he couldn't stand the pain any longer, he killed himself."

Bree's skin had gone cold. Under the table, she knit her fingers together and held on to her own hands. She didn't want to know any more about the ghost. She wanted to simply drop the subject. It didn't have anything to do with her. Yet she found herself asking, "How long ago was that?"

Nola waved a hand in an airy gesture. "At least a hundred years. I'm not precisely sure. He was a cousin of the owner."

So one of Troy's relatives had taken his own life, Bree thought as she ordered herself to sit there calmly. That is, if Nola was telling the truth.

After swallowing, she forced another question past her dry lips. "How do you know?"

Nola appeared to be enjoying herself now. "In the library there's a book on the history of the house. Published by a vanity press. Apparently, one of the former residents fancied himself an author."

Bree nodded. "Can I see the book?"

"Of course. It's big and black with 'Ravencrest' on the spine in gold letters. I've put it on the library table. You can't miss it. But then I also got some firsthand information from the former teacher Miss Carpenter. I believe she had several encounters with the ghost."

Bree couldn't stop herself from leaning forward. "What kind of encounters?"

"Very intense encounters. In the dark of the night. It seems the poor ghost never resolved his feelings. He's still searching for his wife, and when a new woman comes to the house, he seeks her out, hoping she's his lost love."

Bree had gone very still. When Nola didn't continue, she was forced to ask, "And?"

Nola smiled again, the same knowing smile that had grated on Bree's nerves minutes ago. "He's looking for a sexual relationship, although I don't know how a ghost would manage the sex act, do you? But he craves female companionship, so he comes to her room at night, making advances. Kissing and touching, from what Ms. Carpenter said. She was frightened by it, and embarrassed, poor thing. I believe the ghost is what forced her to leave."

"I thought she left because of Dinah. Or did I hear your husband incorrectly last night?" Bree asked carefully.

Nola's face hardened. "He told that to the child because she's such a pest."

Bree was too speechless to respond, but Nola went on smoothly talking. "The ghost is quite sexy."

"You know from personal experience?"

Nola's eyes took on a speculative gleam. "I'll tell you, if you'll tell me."

"I have nothing to tell," Bree insisted, forcing herself to hold the other woman's gaze.

Nola lowered her voice. "Don't you think it would be…stimulating to have a phantom lover? He'd come to your room in the dark. Caress you. Kiss you. Attune you to his touch."

Bree caught her breath, as remembered feelings swept over her. "Don't…"

"Why not? Is it too close to reality?"

Bree held up a hand as if to ward off Nola's inquiry. "No," she averred resolutely, even as her body went rigid in the chair.

FOR WEEKS he had avoided the light of day. But now he took one of his secret routes to the dining room, then stopped short as he listened to the conversation.

Nola was telling Bree about the ghost, and he felt a spurt of anger. She was obsessed with the damn phantom. Too bad he hadn't taken that book out of the library and burned it. Apparently, she'd read the good parts over and over, probably because her husband seemed to have no sexual interest in her.

When she'd first come to Ravencrest, her ghost fantasies had been amusing. But not when she'd started dwelling on the subject with Miss Carpenter.

Now Nola was starting in again with the new teacher, and every instinct urged him to sweep into the room to scare the living daylights out of her. Unfortunately, that would have the same effect on Bree. So he stayed where he was, an unseen listener.

That had been his primary role for the past few weeks. He had kept to the shadows, stayed hidden—unless something roused him to action. For a long time he'd hardly cared what happened one way or the other. Now he felt different. More oriented to the scene playing out in the dining room.

Because of Bree. His gaze was drawn to her. He was entranced by the sight of the sunlight dancing off her golden hair and warming her skin tones. She was wearing a blue sweater and jeans that did nice things for her gentle curves.

He'd stroked those curves last night. Awakened feelings inside himself that he thought were dead. The contact had changed him in ways that he couldn't begin to understand. And he'd come to the dining room this morning eager to see her.

Her tongue flicked across her lips and his attention riveted to the small feminine gesture.

Did she believe that story about the ghost?

Maybe it was best if she did. He'd been drawn to her in the darkness of the night, taken liberties with her. Now he was thinking that he should leave her be. For her sake. Perhaps for his, too. Because the questions she'd asked him had been disturbing, and he wasn't prepared to deal with them. Not yet. Maybe never.

BREE MOISTENED her dry lips, thinking that she couldn't believe this outrageous conversation, even though she'd heard it with her own ears. "Stop," she told Nola. "What are you trying to do?"

"Am I doing something?" Nola feigned innocence.

Then the sound of small feet hurrying along the wooden floor in the hall captured Bree's attention.

Moments later Dinah stepped through the door, her face slightly flushed, her gaze going immediately to Bree. She was still clutching the stuffed kitty that she'd been holding the night before. "I thought you might be gone," she said, her voice slightly breathless.

"Of course I'm here. I'm going to be your teacher. I wouldn't just leave."

The child nodded. "Did you have a good night?"

Bree stared into the little girl's anxious face. The question was startlingly similar to the one Nola had asked, and for a terrible moment, Bree was afraid that Dinah had heard the conversation. Would she have understood it? Bree didn't know. And at the moment, she didn't want to find out.

Taking the question at face value, she answered, "I was so tired, I went right to sleep." Then, switching the subject away from herself, she asked, "So what do you like for breakfast?"

Dinah glanced at Bree's bowl. "Can I have cereal?"

"Of course. Let me help you." Bree half expected Nola to object, but the woman only sat sipping her tea.

As if she knew the child had arrived, Mrs. Martindale bustled in again, a big smile on her face. "Good morning to you," she chirped. "You look like a ray of sunshine."

In response to the housekeeper's greeting, Dinah's face lit up. "Good morning to you!" she returned.

Bree watched the woman and the child. Obviously they enjoyed each other's company. Probably Mrs. Martindale's friendship was helping the little girl cope with life here.

The housekeeper turned to her. "I've been giving Dinah some lessons to do. Of course I'm not a teacher, but I thought I could help her keep up with her studies.''

"Yes, that's good.'' Bree turned to the little girl. "After breakfast you can show me what work you've been doing. Would you like to do that?''

"Yes.''

The housekeeper took away the dirty dishes, then exited the room.

Bree heard Nola make a harrumphing noise. Pushing back her chair, she stood and said, "Well, you two seem to be getting along so well, I assume you'll be having dinner in the schoolroom.''

"That would be fine,'' Bree said.

"One thing you should know. Don't turn your back on her,'' Nola said as she marched out of the room.

Chapter Six

Bree turned quickly, her gaze going to the little girl.

For a moment she caught an expression on the child's face that chilled her. Then the look was gone.

"I'd like my cereal now," Dinah said, her cat clamped under her arm as she moved to the buffet. It was high for her, and she stood on tiptoes to reach for the cereal box.

Bree crossed the room. "Let me help you." She set up Dinah at the table with a bowl of cereal and a glass of juice.

Bree watched the little girl hunch over her breakfast. She wanted to ask what Nola had meant by that cautionary comment. If Bree wasn't mistaken, it sounded as if the woman was deliberately trying to drive a wedge between her and the girl. Or had something bad really happened? Something it was important to know.

Picking up her cup, she went back to the cart and busied herself fixing more tea.

She hoped she looked calm, though her insides were jittery. She'd suddenly thought about a story she'd read in an English literature course in college, *The Turn of the Screw* by Henry James. The similarities to her own situation were startling. It was about a woman who'd been hired as a governess to two parentless children. The boy and girl had seemed nice at first, but then it turned out that they'd been corrupted by a previous governess and her lover whose ghosts came back to haunt the children.

With a shudder, Bree ordered herself to put the tale out of her mind. It was just a ghost story meant to be disturbing, and it had nothing to do with her—and nothing to do with Dinah.

When she turned, she found the child watching her. She forced a smile. "As soon as you're finished, you can show me the way to the schoolroom and we can see what you've been doing."

When Dinah finished breakfast, they retraced the route Bree had taken in the morning, climbing the stairs and then walking down the hall past Bree's room to a door that was just around another corner.

As she crossed the threshold, Dinah turned on the light. It was as though they'd stepped into an old-fashioned, one-room schoolhouse, with blackboards, several dark, wooden, desk-and-chair combinations and a teacher's desk at the front.

Bree walked to the desk and looked through the neatly stacked books and papers. "What are you doing in math?" she asked.

"Addition," Dinah answered promptly, as though eager to be of help.

It felt strange to be in this classroom with only one pupil, Bree thought as she found a sheet with suitable problems and handed them to the girl. "Why don't you do some of these while I look over the materials Miss Carpenter left. Do you have a pencil?"

"Yes."

For the next half hour, while her student worked on the addition problems, Bree studied lesson plans.

But the hair on the back of her neck kept prickling and she couldn't shake the feeling that someone was watching her—just as she was watching Dinah.

Was Troy nearby, in a spot where he could observe them without being seen? Or was somebody else checking up on the schoolroom?

She got up and walked across the polished floor, pretending to inspect the pictures of birds and animals on the bulletin board. She saw no obvious peepholes—or hidden cameras, for that matter. But that didn't mean anything. There could be a microphone in the light fixture, for all she knew.

A small noise made her head turn. Dinah was looking at her.

"Yes?"

"I have to go to the bathroom."

"Sure. You don't have to ask my permission. You can just get up and leave when you have to."

Dinah nodded and slipped out of her seat, taking Alice with her.

Actually, she'd handed Bree an opportunity to snoop around. During the ten minutes she was alone in the room, she tried to make a more thorough inspection of the walls, the fixtures and the floor, but she found nothing.

Dinah returned and went back to work.

The next time she and the girl both looked up, Bree smiled and said, "Shall we have recess? Would you like to go for a walk?"

Dinah looked surprised, but she nodded in agreement then said, "But I'm not supposed to go near the cliffs. Daddy says the edges can be unstable."

"Unstable. That's a big word. Do you know what it means?"

"It means pieces could fall off, and you could fall with them. See, the waves can come up high sometimes and eat away at the dirt. But you don't know it because you can't see the ocean side."

"Well, you do know a lot about it!"

The child glowed with the compliment.

"Thank you for warning me. Can you show me a way out of the house besides the front door?"

Dinah picked up her stuffed animal, then led Bree down a back stairway to a door that opened into the garden. Bree recognized a few of the plants—azaleas and rhododendrons—with a few blooms.

Some beds were weedy. Others had obviously been tended recently. Paving stones wound through the flower beds, then gave way to a gravel path that paralleled the cliff. In the background was a stand of large pine trees—some with broken branches leaning on the ground.

They passed a section of well-tended rosebushes and she paused beside a pinwheel-shaped pink blossom. "Do you know what these are?"

"Some of the Heritage roses. They come from old houses around here. Daddy got them at the botanical garden."

"Oh."

"Daddy likes to garden," Dinah volunteered.

"What other plants does he have besides the roses?"

"We have a very fine collection of heathers and heaths," Dinah answered, obviously repeating what she'd heard a grown-up say.

"You know a lot about the garden," Bree marveled. "More than I ever did."

"Daddy taught me. We have Pacific Coast irises, but they're not blooming now. And fuchsias and California poppies and all kinds of ferns."

The child seemed more animated than at any other time. She must love this garden—perhaps because it represented a connection to her father.

To keep the focus on Troy, Bree asked, "Did your daddy read you *Alice in Wonderland?*"

The child's eyes widened. "How do you know?"

"Well, Alice has a cat named Dinah. I was wondering if that was why you named your kitty Alice?"

"Yes. Daddy thought it was a nice twist," the girl said, and Bree could hear Troy's turn of phrase in the comment.

"I was really disappointed that your daddy wasn't here to meet me. When was the last time you saw him?" Bree asked softly.

The girl scuffed a foot against the gravel of the path. "I can't remember."

The answer sounded like an evasion.

"Did he seem worried about something? Upset?"

Dinah shook her head, and Bree was pretty sure the child was hiding something. She wanted to press for information, but at the same time she understood children pretty well and she sensed the little girl's fragility. She was under a lot of strain living here, and Bree didn't want to make it seem as though the new teacher had come here to ask a lot of personal questions.

In the next moment the child changed the subject abruptly. "Nola told you I was bad," she said in a small voice. "I don't want you to think I'm bad."

"I don't!" Bree answered instantly. "But...do you know what you did to make her mad?"

Silently, Dinah looked down at the tips of her shoes. She heaved a little sigh. "She thinks I threw a dish over the stair railing." Her voice went high and strained. "She thinks I did it on purpose because I wanted to hurt her.

But I didn't drop it on purpose—honest. It slipped out of my fingers when I was leaning over to see who was there and it crashed on the hall floor.''

''And she yelled at you?''

''Yes!'' The answer quavered out on a muffled sob. Tears glistened in her eyes, but she managed to hold them back, and Bree wondered what it must be like for a child to feel as if she had to hide her emotions.

''I'm here to help you,'' she said softly. ''I'm not just your teacher. I'm your friend. You don't have to be afraid anymore.''

Dinah nodded.

''So is there anything else you want to tell me?''

''I…guess not,'' the little girl answered, and Bree suspected there was more she could have said, but that everything wasn't going to come out at once.

''Okay. Then maybe we should go back to the classroom and get a little more done. You can read to me out of your reading book.''

They spent the rest of the morning at work. Then Mrs. Martindale came up to say that lunch was ready.

They all trooped down to the kitchen, where the housekeeper had set out chicken salad sandwiches and bowls of cut-up fruit.

As she ate her sandwich, Bree felt torn. She'd established a rapport with Dinah, and she wanted to keep up the momentum. On the other hand, she had an equally important job—finding out what had happened to the girl's father.

So after lunch she declared an afternoon break, saying she was jet-lagged and needed to rest.

Back in her room, Bree pulled out her suitcase and stopped dead as she looked at the contents. Everything was approximately where she had put it, yet she couldn't help thinking that somebody had searched her things.

Who had been in here?

It would be dangerous to dismiss anyone in the house out of hand. Not even the housekeeper, who seemed nice. She couldn't even omit Troy. One thing was sure: some sexy man was on the loose. Either Troy or a man nobody was talking about. Another thought snuck up on her and she went very still. Lord, could that have been the ghost who'd come to her bed last night? she wondered, suddenly unable to discount Nola's story. No! Either that had been Troy or somebody pretending to be him.

She deliberately pulled her mind away from the ghost and back to the rifled suitcase. The only resident of Ravencrest she could eliminate as being in her room that morning was Dinah. The girl had been with her the whole time. Mentally stopping short, Bree revised that observation. The child hadn't been with her every minute. She'd asked to go to the bathroom, and she'd been gone for ten minutes.

Bree grimaced. She hated suspecting a youngster. But the thought wouldn't go away.

She stared at the clothing for several moments, then removed it so she could get at the bottom of the suitcase. The lining had a special compartment where she'd slipped a few papers.

Opening the Velcro-fastened seam, she pulled out a flat envelope, then extracted the map that Helen had sent her. It showed the floor plan of the house with various rooms marked. The schoolroom was on it. So was Troy's room—a master suite with a bedroom, sitting room, palatial bath and enough closet space for an archduke.

First, she studied the map, then folded it and tucked it into her pocket before getting out something else she

might need—the little tool kit disguised as a mani-
cure set.

Equipped now for prowling, she left her room and
headed for the back stairs that Dinah had shown her. She
had almost reached them when Graves stepped around a
corner, pulling her up short. Her heart leaped into her
throat.

He gave her a considering look. "Where are you going?"

"Um, to my classroom," she improvised.

"You're going the wrong way. It's back there." He
gestured with his hand.

"Yes, thanks. This house is so confusing."

She felt his eyes on her as she backtracked along the
hall. That had been close. Maybe she'd better save her
snooping expedition for another day—when she'd retrieved her gun.

After waiting several minutes, she retraced her steps
to the kitchen and found Mrs. Martindale washing dishes.
She hesitated, wondering if it was safe to ask some questions about Troy and Dinah and the Sterlings. Since she
obviously liked Dinah, the housekeeper might be a good
source of information. But could she be trusted not to
repeat any questions to the Sterlings?

Starting cautiously, Bree said, "I was glad to see that
you have such a good relationship with Dinah."

"She's a sweet little mite."

"And so mature for her age."

Mrs. Martindale rinsed out a large pot and set it in the
dish drainer. "I think she grew up fast when her mother
died."

"What about her father?"

"What about him?"

"Does she get much support from him?"

"He's not in shape to give anyone emotional support at the moment, poor man."

"Yes. Mrs. Sterling said he had a nervous breakdown."

The housekeeper sighed. "He took it hard when his wife died. I think he never got over that. But I don't really feel comfortable talking about my employer."

"Yes, I understand. I really came here to ask if you know where I can find a flashlight."

The housekeeper's gaze turned appraising. "Why do you need one?"

"The light's burned out in my closet," Bree lied again. "And I can't see to put in a new one."

"Then take a bulb with you, too."

"Yes, thanks."

"Just bring me back the flashlight. I like to know where it is, in case we have a power failure."

"Do you have them frequently?" Bree asked.

"Now and again," the housekeeper answered, opening one of the cabinets and producing the requested item.

"Okay. Thanks. I'll give the flashlight back to you at dinner. In the schoolroom, right?"

"At six-thirty."

Bree thanked Mrs. Martindale again, thinking that the woman was either a loyal employee or she had her own reasons for keeping silent about Troy.

When Bree returned to her room, the first thing she did was make sure the closet was empty. Then she checked the bathroom and looked under the bed. When she was sure she was alone, she reentered the closet, unscrewed the bulb, cracked it with the heel of her shoe and dumped it in the trash. After replacing it with the new one, she found the panel that led to the passageway and worked the mechanism. Moments later she was staring down the dark tunnel that led away from her room.

This time she retraced her steps carefully, shining the light on the floor, the walls and even the ceiling. When she judged she was getting close to the place where Troy had saved her from falling, she kept the light focused downward so that she'd be sure to see the chasm in time.

Turning the corner, she found it easily, a shudder racking her as she felt the cold drifting up from the pit. Cautiously she moved toward the edge, inspecting the floor.

The gun could have gone over the edge, but she hadn't heard it fall down there. It was more likely up here. Though she searched for several minutes, she found no sign of the weapon.

Was it in the pit, after all, or had somebody come through here and scooped it up? Who? And how had they gotten in here?

She shone her light along the ledge she'd walked the night before. Now that she could see it better, it looked awfully narrow. The thought of going back there held little appeal. But while she had the light, maybe she could figure out where Troy had disappeared. She inched along the walkway again, breathing a sigh when she made it to the other side.

The rockfall was just as it had been. With the light and her free hand, she carefully inspected every inch of the tunnel. But she could find nothing that looked like a hidden door.

On a sigh, she recrossed the narrow ledge. When she was on firm ground, she turned and stared back at the ledge.

"Dammit, Troy, tell me what's going on!" she

shouted into the darkness. "Tell me how you got in and out of here last night. Tell me what you want from me."

But the only response she heard was her own voice echoing off the dank, dark walls.

Chapter Seven

Bree spent the next few days staying out of the Sterlings' way, and doing what she called "toeing the line," doing nothing that would cause anyone to think she was at Ravencrest for any other purpose than teaching Dinah. During school hours, her focus was as much on getting to know Dinah as on class.

But each night she was free of any duties. She borrowed the leather-bound Ravencrest volume from the library and read about the history of the estate. Nola hadn't made up the story about the ghost. Apparently he *was* in the habit of coming to the rooms of women guests and making sexual advances.

She grimaced. Was that what had happened to her that first night—a sex-starved ghost had foisted his attentions on her? She didn't want to believe that was true. Yet there had been a ghostlike quality to the episode. For instance, she'd never actually seen her visitor. She went back over the subsequent encounter, examining the details, and was unable to definitely prove it had been Troy or the ghost.

If it was the ghost, he hadn't come to her again.

On the other hand, if her visitor had been Troy, which in her heart she truly believed, he had made himself just as scarce. She hadn't seen him again—either at night or during the day. And neither had Dinah. At least that was what the child said when Bree casually asked if she'd talked to her father.

But she did see Mrs. Martindale carrying a covered tray upstairs several times.

"Is that Mr. London's lunch?" Bree asked her once.

The housekeeper gave her a tight nod and hurried up the stairs, confirming the claim that he really was locked in his room.

But he'd gotten out, hadn't he? He'd come to her bed. The longer he failed to make contact with her again, the more her anxiety and feeling of restlessness grew. She was making good progress with Dinah. But she was doing nothing about her primary mission.

Finally, after four days of uncertainty, she knew she had to try to find Troy. If not find him, at least get some information about his situation.

So after lunch, she left Dinah making cookies with Mrs. Martindale and went to see if she could find Graves. When she looked out the window and saw that he was busy raking up leaves in the garden, she decided to take a chance on going to the upper floor again.

FOR DAYS he had watched her from the shadows, knowing where she went and what she did. He watched her with the child. He watched her with the other people in the house.

And in the dark hours of the night he longed to go to her again, to kiss her and to touch her, to feel her response to him, because that contact with her, that response, had transformed him.

He had been numb before she came. He had walked the corridors of Ravencrest and the grounds in a kind of daze, not sure who he was or why he was here. He remembered anger. He remembered pain. Physical pain. And the pain of betrayal, as well. She hadn't wiped away those emotions, but she had changed him for the better. She had that power.

She had made him remember things he hadn't even known he'd forgotten. There were still missing pieces, but now he had access to facts, feelings. He should thank her for that, even though some of it was agonizing. So bad, in fact, that he understood why he had banished entire episodes of his life from his mind.

On the other hand, a lot of it was good. Like the summer when he'd known he was falling in love with her. He spent long hours now reliving those sweet memories. He had his favorites. Of course, he liked remembering how he'd awakened her sexually. How he'd kissed her and touched her and felt the thrill of her response to him. But there were other memories that were just as vivid.

Queenie, one of the bitches on the ranch, had given birth to a litter of buff-and-brown puppies. He remembered how Bonnie had cooed over those little wiggling bodies, how she'd cuddled them in her arms and stroked her face against their baby-soft fur.

Of course, she was a different person now. Not as passive or as naive. He liked the change. Yet at the same time some inner part of him was afraid to trust her. For a long time he had trusted nobody. Not even himself. Well, nobody besides the child. She'd been like a bright beam of light shining into his dark existence.

Then Bree had come here, too. But what if she left as suddenly as she had come?

So he held himself back, silently vowing that the next time they met, she must come to him.

He wasn't certain why he needed that reassurance.

Maybe it was a kind of test. If she wanted the same thing he did—if she wanted it badly enough—then she would prove it to him.

So he kept watch. When he saw her slip the small box into her pocket, he felt dizzy with a kind of heart-pounding anticipation.

BREE TOOK A STEADYING breath as her hand closed around the kit in her pocket. In the days since her first aborted try to navigate the halls of Ravencrest, she'd memorized the map Helen had sent her. All she had to do now was head for the stairs.

As she made her way up, she kept expecting to feel a hand clamp on to her shoulder. But nobody accosted her.

In the upper hall she paused to get her bearings, then headed straight for the master suite. When she reached the door, she carefully tried the knob.

It was locked.

"Troy?" she called, pitching her voice low. He didn't answer, but from the other side of the door came a burst of sound.

Music. Music that made her throat tighten as she recognized the song. A Rod Stewart standard.

Pressing her ear to the door, she listened intently, trying to make sure she wasn't hearing things. But it was Rod Stewart, all right, singing "Maggie May." Helen had been into Rod Stewart the summer she'd visited, and she'd played him constantly. Bree and Troy had laughed about the ubiquitous presence of the gravel-voiced tenor. But they'd also enjoyed the songs. In fact, more than one night, out on the porch, they'd danced to the music before switching back to slow numbers.

Now, like a ghost from the past, the song drifted toward her through the door, as though Troy was welcoming her to his room. "Maggie May" was one of Stewart's best-known works—an edgy ballad about disillusionment and a relationship breaking up. The cut finished and another song picked up.

"Tonight's the Night." She caught her breath as the new words wrapped themselves around her. This one was quite different. It wasn't a lament; it was about a couple getting ready to make love for the first time.

She pressed her cheek against the hard wood, listening, remembering that she'd imagined herself and Troy as the two people getting comfortable with each other, their thoughts drifting toward the bedroom.

"Troy," she said, her voice soft.

Was it her imagination or did she hear someone speak her name from the other side of the door.

"Troy?" she called again, this time a little louder.

She let her mind drift into a little fantasy. He'd been waiting for her to come up here and he had played the music when he knew she was on her way.

That was nonsense, she told herself. Impossible. Yet she felt her hands shaking as she got out the tool kit. The lock wasn't complicated. All she had to do was insert a pick in the doorknob hole and press.

The mechanism clicked and she turned the knob. Feeling as if she was doing something illegal, she stepped quickly into the room, knowing she might be taking a terrible chance.

If Troy was in here, if he was dangerous, then she should turn around and leave. But she didn't believe Nola's story about his having a nervous breakdown and being locked in. So she pulled the door closed. Hesitating several more seconds, she made another decision and snapped the lock behind her.

With the room dimly lit, she could see very little at

first. But she was instantly aware of Troy's scent. After-shave and man. At least it was the scent of the man who had come to her bed four nights ago.

She breathed deeply, then called his name as she'd done on the other side of the door.

He didn't answer, but she knew he had been here recently. Her heart leaped. Locating a lamp on the stand near the door, she switched it on then eagerly looked around the room. Her eyes bounced from the reupholstered vintage sofa and chair near the window to the beautifully refinished cabinet pieces.

Eagerness turned to disappointment when she saw only furniture.

The music was coming from a small stereo that sat on a marble-topped chest. Beside it a set of shelves held dozens of CDs and tapes—everything from classical to jazz to popular groups and artists, she saw as she skimmed the titles.

On the wall above the stereo were framed pictures. Bree's stomach clenched as she caught sight of Troy. He was the same man she remembered from the summer in Montana. Smiling and vital, only a little older. There were several pictures of him with Dinah, and there was a family portrait of Troy, Dinah and a smiling, dark-haired woman who must have been his wife, Grace.

Another picture of Troy standing alone had been taken at the ranch, she knew, from the backdrop of the mountains. Seeing him in that familiar setting made her heart squeeze.

She pivoted away from the pictures, seeing shelves that held biographies, novels and volumes that he must have used as references in his work. Interspersed with them were various objects: a child's stacking toy, a small box of polished green stone, a rounded black-and-white rock from the beach.

Magazines were spread out on the table in front of the sofa, current editions she saw when she inspected the dates—but that didn't necessarily prove he'd been here recently. She'd like to see one of those trays Mrs. Martindale had carried upstairs—with dirty dishes on it, indicating that he'd actually eaten a meal in this room recently. Or a stack of newly opened mail.

It looked as though someone had set out the books and magazines as props. Someone who didn't feel Troy's presence here and wanted to make it appear as if he'd been in the room.

Crossing to the darkened bedroom, she took a quick peek inside and saw no one. The bed was made. A plaid shirt was thrown across the arm of a mission-style chair and a pair of black leather slippers sat beside it.

In the bathroom, toilet articles were set out on shelves, and a razor sat on the sink.

She could imagine Troy standing there that morning, getting ready for the day. But both the sink and the tub were clean and bone dry, as though neither had been used recently.

The mixed signals made her hands clench. It felt as though he could step into the room at any moment. Yet at the same time she wondered if he'd been here in weeks.

"If you're here, come out," she said, making each word clear and distinct. "And if you don't want me rifling through your private papers, say so because Helen sent me here to get information, and it looks like snooping is my only option now."

Maybe that *was* what he wanted. Maybe he wanted her

to discover things that he couldn't or wouldn't voice to her.

When he didn't object to her stated plan, she walked back to the desk and sat on the swivel chair. Opening the middle drawer, she saw office items, all neatly arranged in compartments and small boxes.

After a quick glance over her shoulder, she began opening other drawers. There were various papers: paid bills, junk mail that he'd shoved into a pile, a letter from a heating and cooling company asking if he wanted to keep up his extended warranty on the furnace and air-conditioning system.

Despite her spoken warning, poking through Troy's private life made her stomach knot. Still, she forced herself to continue the search.

In another drawer were directions for various appliances. Below them were several photocopied statements from a brokerage firm. The name of one company on the report caught her eye and she sucked in a quick breath. Enteck.

Troy had bought Enteck stock? She looked at the bottom line. When Troy had filed away these statements, the company had been doing well. In fact, it had been the leader in the energy field eighteen months ago. Then it had shocked the market by filing for bankruptcy. The stock was virtually worthless now, and from the looks of the statements from the brokerage firm, Troy had sunk a lot of his fortune into the company.

Bree returned the papers to the drawer and rocked back in the chair.

Was that Troy's problem? He'd made a fatal business decision and lost his fortune. And now...

Several thoughts leaped to her mind. He was hiding out from his creditors. He'd tried to recoup his losses—

and gotten into even worse trouble. His financial problems had given him a nervous breakdown. Or was that just the story he'd put out so people would leave him alone?

If only she could ask him!

"Troy!" she said in exasperation as she marched back to the bedroom.

Impulsively, she crossed the Oriental rug and eased onto the bed, staring at the quilted surface of the spread as she smoothed her hand across the blue-and-brown fabric.

As she sat there, the feeling of being watched was so strong that her head jerked up and she looked quickly around.

Her gaze zinged to the closet, where the door was open a crack.

"Troy?"

He could be hiding in there, she suddenly realized. He could have been hiding and watching her all along. And Nola had said he was dangerous.

The smart thing was to get out of the room—if she believed Nola's story. But she didn't trust the woman. After all, Troy had proved himself by saving her life the first night she'd been at the estate. Troy, or someone who used the same aftershave as the man who lived in this room.

Her heart had started pounding wildly in her chest. Before she could change her mind, she stood, recrossed the room and pulled the closet door open.

Disappointment and relief warred within her when she saw nobody was standing by the door.

Still, it would be possible to hide in here. The closet was large and cavernous, at least ten feet by ten feet—a small bedroom in any other house. The light in back of her was low, making the rows of hanging shirts and jackets dark and shadowy.

Feeling along the wall, she found the light switch and flipped it up, but nothing happened. Apparently the bulb was burned out. So wouldn't Troy have replaced it if he really was living in this room?

A prickle of unease made goose bumps on her arms. Behind her, in the sitting area, the music swelled, and she jumped. This time Rod Stewart was singing "Do You Think I'm Sexy?"

"Stop it!"

All at once, the aroma of his spicy aftershave was stronger than before and she sensed him standing so close to her that she could reach out and touch him—if she knew where he was.

Her throat closed, her mouth went dry. Somehow she managed to get out one syllable: his name.

Her pulse pounded in her ears as she waited for an answer.

Eons passed before he said, "Yes. I tried to stay away from you. But I couldn't. Not after you came up here."

His voice was stronger than she'd heard it up till now, and a mixture of joy, relief and fear flared in her breast.

She started to turn toward him, but he stepped quickly behind her and his strong hands clasped her shoulders, forcing her to remain in place.

She tried to slip from his hold, but he was strong and easily kept her where she was. Her hands clenched and unclenched in frustration. "Troy, let me see you."

"You can't." Again he spoke with force.

"Did something happen to your face? Is it scarred? Is that why you're staying out of sight? Is that why I haven't seen you or heard from you in days?"

When he didn't answer, her stomach knotted. "Don't you trust me?" she whispered.

"I can't trust anyone," he answered, and this time his voice was harsh and grating.

All the questions bottled up inside her burst out. "Oh, Lord, Troy. What happened? What's wrong? Nola told me you're supposed to be locked in here. Is that true? Or is she lying to cover something up? And if you're not locked in, are you using another secret passage? Please, you have to tell me."

Again she tried to turn so that she was facing him, but he only clamped his fingers more tightly onto her shoulders, pulling her back so that her body rested firmly against his.

"We can talk here," he said. "Like this."

Talk, she thought, trying not to focus on the sensation he was creating. He was warm and solid and strong. The man she remembered from their summer together. He'd been clever then, he was more clever now. He knew exactly how to distract her, but she wasn't going to let him get away with it. "Answer my questions. Did they lock you in your room?"

He gave a short laugh. "Yeah, I heard that story. It's a lie."

The assurance buoyed her. He wasn't locked in here. Yet what about the rest of it? "But you're in trouble. Is it financial trouble, or something worse?" she pressed.

There was a long hesitation, during which every muscle in her body tensed.

"Something worse," he finally answered.

When he didn't elaborate, she almost screamed, "You have to tell me!"

He made a strangled sound, then answered. "Okay. I killed Grace."

Bree gasped. "Oh, no, Troy. That can't be true."

"I killed Grace," he said again, as though the memory had just surfaced in his mind and he was trying to decide what to do with it.

"No!" she repeated. "You loved your wife."

"Did I?"

"Helen told me how happy you were."

"Then Helen was mistaken. Grace and I had problems from the start."

She struggled to process what he was saying, even as she tried to twist out of his arms, but he held her where she was.

In a shaky voice she asked, "If you didn't love her, why did you marry her?"

"I got her pregnant."

"Oh." The one clipped syllable was all she could manage.

"And then I killed her."

"How?"

"In the car."

"You mean, an accident?"

He dragged in a breath and let it out. "Technically."

"Then—"

Ruthlessly, he cut her off. "We were having one of our fights. At the end we were fighting all the time about how much money she was spending on the house. I told her we had to cut back or she'd bankrupt us, and she just kept pouring on the money—maybe because the house had become a symbol to her." He stopped and heaved a sigh. "I can't always remember that night. Sometimes it goes away and leaves me alone."

He wouldn't permit her to turn and hold him close. All she could do was reach back and close her hands gently over his forearms, silently lending him her strength. He bent his head, pressed his cheek against her hair.

"Let me help you," she murmured. "Tell me what happened."

He was silent for several moments, then continued. "It was foggy, and the road was slick. She was yelling at me, and she took a curve too fast. The car hit the rocks, then bounced over the cliff. I was thrown out—I guess because I'd forgotten to buckle my seat belt. She went into the ocean with the car."

"Oh, my God." Bree gasped. "Troy, you didn't kill her! She was driving."

"But we were fighting. She was focused on me, not on the road. If I'd kept my mouth shut and just let her concentrate on what she was supposed to be doing, it wouldn't have happened."

"You can't blame yourself."

"The hell I can't!"

"Troy." This time his name sighed out of her. She felt his chest rising and falling, felt him match the rhythm of his breathing to hers.

"Thank you for telling me," she murmured.

"You have the right to know."

"Why?"

"Because in Montana, after you left, I met Grace. And I was lonely. We…got close too quickly. She wasn't like you. She wasn't sweet and innocent. Then she told me she was going to have a baby. I couldn't leave her like that. Do you understand?"

"Yes," she breathed. Finally, after all these years, she did understand why he'd married someone else when it had looked as if they'd been heading toward something incredibly good.

She heard the anguish in his voice as he continued.

"God knows, I tried to make the marriage work. For a little while things were okay. And she gave me an incredible gift—Dinah."

"Oh, yes."

"Then…Grace and I started getting on each other's nerves. We should have gotten divorced. But she told me she'd take Dinah away and I believed her. She would have done it to punish me."

She heard his shallow breathing. He had just confessed his deepest sins and she knew he was waiting for her reaction.

She clutched at his forearms, angled her head so she could soothe her cheek against his shoulder.

"Punish you for what?"

"Taking away the lifestyle she'd come to love."

"Then don't blame yourself," she murmured.

His confession had released her from her own secret guilt. She'd wanted this man for so long, and she'd told herself over and over that it was wrong because he was happily married. She'd tried to substitute other relationships, but her memory of him had always gotten in the way. Now he had told her the truth, and she knew she hadn't imagined the feelings between them all those years ago.

Still, a tiny kernel of doubt niggled at her. The last time she'd talked to him, he'd claimed he couldn't remember the recent past. Now he had come out with this fully formed story. How much of what he'd said was true?

She wanted to believe him. And there was one thing she absolutely had to believe. She had missed him all these years, and he was telling her that he had missed her, too.

More than that, he needed her. She knew that if he let

her, she could help him heal his soul. By allowing her to share his sadness and his guilt, and by building on the feelings that she'd struggled so hard to repress because she'd thought they were wrong.

She stood there, leaning back against him, just breathing, just tuning herself to something fundamental that seemed to grow from the contact between them.

She had been frightened in this house, unsure. But now that she was with him, and they were actually communicating, everything seemed different.

He had the power to make it different.

He bent his head and brushed her hair aside, so his lips could find the tender place where her jawline met her neck. She had told herself they were simply giving each other comfort, but there was no denying the sensual undercurrent to his touch.

His lips inched upward and she heard a small sigh ease from her own lips.

She knew he heard, too, because the sound led his finger to her lips, where he touched her with a feather-light stroke.

Her neck arched, giving him better access. He was weaving a sensual web around her again, the way he'd done so easily in her bedroom. He was a magician who had learned just the right tricks to bring her under his spell.

She struggled to fight the fog wafting through her brain. She told herself that she had to make herself think, make him keep communicating in words instead of touches. But now that everything had changed, she had lost the will to protest. Instead, she opened her mouth so he could stroke the sensitive tissue of her lips. Then, with a small sound, she went from passive to aggressive, trapping his finger between her teeth, nibbling on him, playing with the skin.

Behind her, he caught his breath, and she felt as though the rules of the encounter had changed.

"Let me turn around," she pleaded, the request coming out high and breathy.

"I've decided it's better like this."

She'd been drifting on a cloud of sensuality. Now the impact of his words was almost a physical blow.

"You decided! Do you make all the decisions?"

"I have to."

Before she could demand an explanation, a noise in the hall made them both go rigid.

Bree's heart leaped into her throat. "Somebody's here," she gasped.

He cursed under his breath and moved away from her, leaving her standing alone in the closet.

In the next moment the door flew open and she found herself facing Nola Sterling.

"I thought I heard music in here! First I find you scrabbling around behind a curtain in the hall, now you're in the master suite! What in the hell are you doing in Mr. London's bedroom?" Nola demanded, standing in the doorway, her hands balled into fists and planted on her hips. Her voice was controlled, but her narrow face reflected a bad case of nerves.

"Is this Mr. London's bedroom?" Bree asked, using her sweet little Southern belle voice.

"You know damn well it is! That's why you came here. Don't hide in the damn closet."

Nola backed up to give Bree room to follow. She took a step forward but remained a few inches inside the closet doorway, struggling to look innocent, even as her mind scrambled for some other explanation. "I was exploring the house. I was in a lot of rooms. You just happened to find me here," she heard herself saying, lying through her teeth again. Lord, she was getting good at lying, she thought, hating the way she was bending her moral code. "This place is so stunning. I wanted to look around. I didn't know what room it was. And since you told me Mr. London has been violent, I certainly wouldn't have come in here if I'd known it was his room."

Nola cocked her head, staring at her. "You don't have permission to explore the house. You're supposed to be with the little girl. And this room is always locked. How did you get in?"

Bree dredged up a befuddled look. "It wasn't locked," she said, her voice still all innocence.

Nola's eyes narrowed. "You're saying you just walked in?"

"Yes."

"And did you turn on the music?"

"No. I'm not very mechanical. I don't fool with other people's CD players."

"If you didn't turn it on, who did?"

Bree raised her chin slightly. "Maybe that sexy ghost you told me about."

Nola blanched, and Bree knew she'd scored a point, although she couldn't follow the logic of it.

But the woman recovered quickly. "I don't think so," she said firmly. "Let's get back to you. You claim that before you came in here, you were in other rooms. Describe them."

"Which…which ones?" Bree hedged. "There are so many."

"Start with the one next door on the right. That is, if you want to keep your job."

Chapter Eight

Bree had no idea what the room on the right looked like. She was desperately floundering for something to say when a voice whispered in her ear. Troy's voice, coming from behind her, low and husky, sending a shiver over her skin.

"The room on the right is a little sitting room. There are couches and a television set. The room next to that is another bedroom. It's bright and cheery—yellow and white. There's a cut-glass dish of potpourri on the dresser. If she asks you about anything else, tell her you saw too much to remember it all."

She resisted the impulse to look over her shoulder, to see where he was. His voice had come to her on a whisper, and she wondered if Nola had heard him, too. Yet the woman gave no sign that she was aware of anyone else in the room besides Bree.

"Quit stalling!"

Bree swallowed, took a step out of the closet, then repeated the information Troy had fed her, watching Nola's face relax somewhat.

"All right. So Helen London hired a first-class snoop. You looked in several rooms," she conceded. "But that doesn't explain how you got in here."

Bree let a look of distress wash over her face. "Nobody said I was confined to one part of the house. And with this room—I told you, the door was unlocked. I just turned the knob," she said.

"That's impossible."

Bree watched Nola. The woman was acting more and more agitated. She looked as if she were standing on a hill of sand and it was slipping out from under her feet.

"I'd like you out of this room," Nola snapped. "That's an order, not a request. If I find you in here again, you will be dismissed."

"Okay, sure," Bree said weakly.

She would have liked to ask Nola why *she* had come up to Troy's room. She didn't have a tray with her, so she wasn't delivering a meal. But she knew that asking any question would be a bad idea. Instead she said, "I'm sorry if I stepped on anyone's toes."

Somehow she kept herself from looking back toward the closet. She wanted to plunge inside and start pushing clothing aside, so she could look for Troy—or for a hidden passage where he'd escaped after giving her the information that had gotten her off the hook with Nola. But she wasn't going to get a chance to do that now. Or later, either, since she'd just been warned that this room was off-limits. And if she got caught here, it was all over.

They stepped into the hall, and Nola clicked the lock before pulling the door shut. She waited while Bree made her way along the hall and down the steps before marching away in the other direction.

Bree kept walking, her steps measured but her mind whirling. Now that she was alone, the intensity of the conversation with Troy slammed into her.

He'd said his marriage hadn't worked out. He'd said he felt guilty about his wife's death.

Lord, she'd never known that he'd gotten Grace pregnant in Montana. Never known that was the reason he hadn't sought her out after she'd left to go home to take care of Mom.

She might have headed for the kitchen to see if Dinah was still there, since she'd just been reminded she was supposed to be teaching the little girl, but she needed a few minutes to herself.

Because the farther she got from Troy's room, the more things that had seemed so clear were turning muddy again. Troy had given her reasons for his not contacting her after she'd left. In effect, he'd spun a story—a story she wanted to believe—about why he hadn't gotten back together with her.

He'd also told her about the car accident. But that wasn't really relevant to what was going on now. It didn't explain why he was hiding out—unless the police wanted to question him about the events of that night. Nobody had made that suggestion. And the accident didn't explain what the Sterlings were up to.

Now that she was alone, she felt her chest tighten. She was scared and confused and in over her head on so many levels.

He said his wife was dead. Yet he was the one who kept appearing and then vanishing like a ghost. Bree stopped short and looked over her shoulder, feeling torn in two. She wanted desperately to go back to his room to make a thorough search of the closet—to find out how he'd disappeared and how he'd spoken to her without Nola seeing him. But under the circumstances, that was simply too much of a risk.

She sighed. When she and Troy had been talking together, he'd done a skillful job of directing the conversation, yet there were so many questions left unanswered.

She didn't know if that was because he was hiding incriminating details from her or because his memory was impaired and he didn't have all the facts.

Whatever the reason, she knew she needed help, from either the Light Street Detective Agency or Randolph Security. She should have told them she was coming or called when she'd assessed the situation here. But she'd been putting it off for two good reasons: first, she knew she was going to catch hell for coming to Ravencrest on her own, and second, over the past few days, she'd convinced herself she was handling things. Now she knew she'd been fooling herself about that second item, and she was willing to throw herself on the mercy of her friends and colleagues back home.

Once she'd made the decision, it was all she could do to keep from running to get her cell phone. Instead she made her way down the stairs at a reasonable pace, then stepped into her room.

She'd left her purse in the bottom right dresser drawer. Pulling it out, she began searching for the phone.

When she couldn't find it, she crossed the room on shaky legs and turned her purse upside down, dumping the contents onto the bed. She saw her wallet, her keys, two pens and an assortment of her belongings, but no phone. Carefully she checked all the interior pockets. The phone—her connection to the outside world—was gone.

She couldn't have lost it; she was sure it had been in her purse when she'd arrived. She took a quick look around the room—under the bed, in her suitcase, under other pieces of furniture.

The cell phone was definitely missing.

Taken by the same person who'd searched her suitcase the day after she arrived, she reasoned. Or maybe the ghost had done it.

All at once she felt the walls close in on her, felt her heart pound in her chest, and it was difficult to take in a full breath.

She'd had panic attacks in the past, when she'd been really worried about her mom, and she recognized the symptoms.

Calm down, she ordered herself. *Don't do this. It's not going to help. Don't let this house and the people here get the better of you,* she repeated over and over, because deep inside she knew that she couldn't afford to fall apart. The old Bonnie Brennan might have crawled into bed and pulled the covers over her head. But not Bree Brennan.

By force of will, she brought herself under control, keeping her breathing slow and even. When she was feeling more self-possessed, she thought about the phone situation at Ravencrest. There wasn't one in the kitchen or in Troy's room, either. If she wanted to make a call, she'd have to ask Nola or find the estate office.

And she certainly wasn't going to be making a call to the Light Street Detective Agency in front of Nola or Abner Sterling.

Where was Abner, anyway? she asked herself. She'd seen him only once, throwing a tantrum in the hall. Maybe he was really the guy confined to his room, and he'd gotten out the night she arrived.

She sighed, thinking that she was letting her imagination run away with her.

She clenched her teeth, then deliberately relaxed, trying to decide on a course of action.

Someone had made sure she couldn't use her cell phone. Maybe the thing to do was to drive into town and use a public phone.

She glanced toward the window. Clouds had blown up

since she and Dinah had walked outside that morning. The sky looked dark and threatening.

But suddenly it had become important to get off the estate now. Quickly she pulled on her light raincoat, then hurried along the hall and down the stairs. As she stepped outside, the wind almost tore the door from her hand and she had to drag it closed. Turning, she watched the trees and bushes shiver violently in the wind. Was it just the wind? Or some supernatural force giving her a warning?

Supernatural force! Lord, she was the one losing her mind.

Taking a deep breath, she dashed to her rental car, inserted the key in the lock and opened the door. Once she was safely inside, she breathed out a small sigh. She'd shut away the evil influences from the house. She was safe.

Leaning back she closed her eyes for a moment, simply absorbing the sudden feeling of security. But when she inserted the key in the ignition and turned it, nothing happened.

Nothing happened on the second or third try, either.

Reaching down, she released the hood latch, then climbed out, pushed up the hood and stared at the engine.

Of course, her knowledge of machinery would fit into a pillbox. What did she expect—that someone had disabled the car and left a big red sign explaining what they'd done?

For several minutes she stared helplessly at the unfamiliar collection of parts. Then she slammed the hood closed and turned in a circle. The wind had died down and the clouds had thinned, so that the atmosphere didn't seem quite so ominous.

Still, she saw bushes sway. Not from the wind. Someone was standing about twenty-five feet away, watching her.

Graves? He seemed to be outside a lot. Had he done something to her car?

"Graves?" she called.

He didn't answer. Of course.

It was mind-blowing to realize that she'd been on this estate less than a week and so many things had happened. She was tired of people doing things to her, tired of getting caught in one crisis after another and being forced to respond—and not on her own terms.

Perhaps she was still reacting to the earlier confrontation with Nola. Then she'd forced herself to be polite and cooperative because she'd been caught in Troy's room. But this was different. She'd been in her own car, minding her own business. Now she was mad enough to march toward the bushes, her hands on her hips.

"Come out of there and face me, you coward!" she bellowed.

In response, the watcher backed up, and she got a good look at him. It wasn't Graves. It was the man who had been staying out of her way since that first night. Abner Sterling.

He stood for a moment, staring at her. Then he turned and started walking rapidly along the cliff.

"Come back here!" she called, her anger boiling up, spiraling out of control. She'd conquered the panic attacks, but now she was swept in another direction by her feeling of helplessness. When he failed to heed her order, she stomped after him, unwilling to let him disable her car and run away.

"Come back here, you coward," she screamed as she reached the margin of the garden area. Beyond were the headlands, the stretch of wild grass and low plants bordering the cliffs.

Sterling kept going, picking up speed so that he was rushing along the seaside path in an awkward run. Recklessly, she charged after him, her hair streaming behind her in the breeze blowing off the ocean, her pants' legs catching against twigs and thorns that overhung the path.

She came face-to-face with her foolhardy behavior when Sterling suddenly stopped short and turned to confront her. She stared at him, seeing his face screw itself into a contorted mask.

"Why are you following me?" he shouted across the hundred feet of space that separated them. His hands were clenched, the way his wife's had been earlier. Only, compared to him, Nola had seemed restrained. Abner looked as if he was about to explode.

"You did something to my car," she said lamely, suddenly wondering what she had planned to do if she caught up with him. Force him into a confession? Yeah, sure. He was at least a hundred pounds heavier and a head taller than she was.

His voice sounded outraged as he answered, "I did not! Where do you get off saying something like that?"

"You were watching to see what happened," she shouted back.

"I was outside. I saw you go to your car. I wanted to see what you were up to."

"You can assume I was going to drive it!"

"I'm not going to assume a damn thing. Not anymore! Not with what's been going on around here."

"What does that mean?"

"You stay here long enough and you'll find out what it's like living in an insane asylum with the inmates on the loose."

She stared at him, trying to work her way through his statements, starting with his comments about the car and progressing to what sounded like paranoid fear.

As she stood in the middle of the path he started back toward her, his features distorted, his skin flushed. His jaw was working; his arms were rigid. His eyes were slitted. He looked like a little kid about to have a tantrum and she had no idea what he would do if he caught up with her.

Turning swiftly on her heel, she began to run back toward the house. Behind her, she heard his footsteps gaining on her. He was going to catch her and she was pretty sure he wasn't planning to give her a warm handshake.

Real fear grabbed her by the throat. The headlands were like a wild, open meadow, with steep cliffs on one side.

The house was too far away to offer help. And if Abner wanted to pitch her over the edge of the cliff, he could just go back home and nobody would find her—maybe for days.

As she decided what to do, a voice suddenly called her name.

"Bree. Over here!"

Her head swung toward a stand of trees about twenty-five yards away.

Was that Troy?

It seemed like his voice, but she couldn't be sure. Not out on the headlands where the wind blowing off the sea distorted all sound. And not just the wind. Almost below the level of consciousness, she heard a deep, rhythmic drumming. A throbbing sound that increased as she altered her course and headed for the trees, detouring around a decaying fallen trunk.

A little while ago she'd questioned Troy's motives. Now she didn't hesitate at the edge of the grove. Without missing a step, she dove into the shadows below the branches.

Immediately she was plunged into a world quite different from the open headlands. What looked to her like Spanish moss hung in curtains from the branches overhead. And smaller, compact moss and lichens clung to the tree trunks, creating a place that might have been an old Druid grove.

It was dark here. And mysterious. The forest primeval. But more than that, a kind of charged energy seemed to gather in the air, like a current of electricity building from a storm.

The humming sound increased, swelling like the beat of a giant drum—or a human heart.

It competed with the sound of the wind, which was blowing not off the ocean but in a circular whirlwind that moved among the trees, picking up bits of moss, pine needles, bark and plants that grew under the trees.

Bree shaded her eyes, gawking at the small tornado that never moved beyond the confines of the grove.

Was she hallucinating? Looking back over her shoulder, she realized that Abner Sterling had stopped short about thirty yards away. He, too, was staring fixedly at the whirl of debris.

She heard a gasp escape him. He backed away, slowly at first and then more rapidly. Turning, he began running along the cliff again toward the house.

Bree watched him retreat, breathing out a little sigh. Then she turned back toward the darkness under the trees.

The deep beating seemed to crest. The spiral of pine needles and debris was about fifty feet from her, staying steady, in one place, and as she stared at the roiling current, her eyes widened. Through the curtain of the whirling matter, she thought she saw a human form. A man. The whirlwind obscured the outlines of his body. And he was shadowed by the mass of tree branches blocking out the sun, so that she couldn't be absolutely sure that the image wasn't some trick of the light or the swirling debris.

She remained transfixed, straining her eyes, trying to make out details. As far as she could see, he was about six feet tall and well-muscled, dressed in jeans and a dark flannel shirt—like the one laid out on the chair in Troy's room.

She called his name.

The only answer was the throbbing rhythm that remained as an underlying sound and the swirling of the air currents as they flung bits of debris against the tree trunks.

Then, all at once, the wind ceased, as though it had never been, and there was utter silence around her. Even the drum had stopped.

''Troy!'' she tried once more. She seemed to be always calling his name, she thought, with uneven success.

Without conscious thought, she hurried farther under the canopy of trees, making for the spot where she'd seen him last.

Her eyes were focused ahead of her and she wasn't watching where she was going. Her foot caught against a hidden tree root and she stumbled, pitching forward. She was going to hit the ground; her arms came up to break her fall. But before disaster struck, strong arms captured her and set her back on her feet—the way they'd done when she'd almost stumbled into the pit.

Though she didn't know how it happened, Troy was

standing behind her. She caught her breath, leaning into the solid wall of his body.

"Troy."

"Yes, it's me."

She'd come out of the house thinking it was dangerous to trust him. Now she closed her eyes, resting quietly against him. He was strong, capable of defending her from all danger. At least it felt that way here in this secret grove.

Time had no meaning in this place. And it seemed that the ordinary laws of the universe failed to penetrate under the branches that blocked out the light above her. It might have been seven years ago, when they'd first met, first gotten close.

So much had happened since then. But here she could pretend for a little while that none of it had transpired. Because she desperately wished that were true. If only they hadn't been torn apart all those years ago, everything would be different.

Troy pulled her into an even darker spot, where tree trunks and low branches created a private place, just for the two of them. As he had before, he kept her close, his hands moving over her shoulders, down her arms, making her skin tingle.

Somehow, out here in the open air, he felt more real, more solid than he had at any of their previous meetings, and when he spoke, his voice was strong and decisive. Yet his words broke the spell she'd let herself fall under.

"You're safe in the grove. They're afraid to come here."

"Why?"

"They sense my presence in this place."

"Troy, please, let's get out of here. Away from the estate."

His hands opened and closed on her arms. "I can't."

There was a kind of bleak anguish in his voice now. She might have tried to turn. But she knew from experience that he wanted her to stay where she was.

"You have to take Dinah and leave. Get her out of here to somewhere safe. Promise me you'll do that."

"I…"

"Promise."

"Yes. All right. I'll take her away. If you can't do it yourself."

"Thank you."

"Troy, what's going on? Did Nola and Abner Sterling do something to you?"

She heard him drag in a breath and let it out in a frustrated rush. "I don't know. There are still things I don't know!"

Her heart turned over as she heard the frustration in his voice. But still, she needed as much information as she could get. "You told me about the accident, but something else happened later," she said. "You were hurt, weren't you? Can you tell me about it?"

"No."

"You don't remember?"

She felt him shake his head.

"But you remember some things!"

"Yes. If I could answer all your questions, I would."

"Would you?"

"Yes."

She desperately wanted to believe him. Trying a different tack, she asked, "Where are you staying? Somewhere in the house?"

"Out here."

"Out here?"

"It's as good a place as any."

"You have a shelter? A safe place?"

"I have what I need."

Again, she wanted to make him give her details, but she was pretty sure it would only frustrate him more.

Striving for a positive note she said, "You sound stronger."

"You're making me stronger."

Her eyes blinked open. "Me? How?"

"When I hold you, I feel your strength. When I touch you like this."

His breath warm on her skin, he took her tender earlobe between his strong teeth and delicately played with it.

"Oh!" Her eyes drifted closed again because she wanted to concentrate on nothing besides him.

"I love the way you respond to me. You always responded to me so sweetly."

She couldn't answer. She could only prove his point by arching into the tingling caress. Just a small thing, his mouth on her ear, but she had never felt anything so erotic.

He continued his playful attentions, down the sensitive column of her neck, teasing her with his lips, his teeth, his tongue.

No longer holding her in place, his hands slid down her sides, tracing the shape of her hips. Then, slowly, he slid them back upward, along her ribs and then to the undersides of her breasts, where he stroked along the rounded swells.

It was only a light touch. Maybe the lightness of it was what drove her mad. She felt her nipples contract to tight points, heard her own indrawn breath.

"Please," she moaned, her head falling back against his shoulder. All those years ago he had been careful with her. Respectful. Kept his hands from straying to intimate places.

Now he had changed the rules. Slowly, he drove her closer to insanity, his hands inched upward, finding the undersides of her nipples and touching her just there. Stroking back and forth, the light contact more stimulating than if he had taken her firmly in hand.

Her whole body tuned itself to him, to that slight but commanding caress. Breath sawed in and out of her lungs as she waited, suspended in an unbearable anticipation of need. And when his fingers finally circled her nipples, she cried out with the intensity of it.

She was weightless, boneless, unable to stand without the support of his rock-hard body behind her. One of his arms circled her waist. The other worked the buttons of her blouse, opening them one by one, exposing her skin to the cool air—another distinct sensation on her heated flesh.

He pushed the shirt to the sides, under her raincoat, then tugged the cups of her bra down so that he could free her breasts to the air and his touch.

She let him do what he wanted. Let him tease and torture her, out here in the open air, under the branches of the trees.

One hand slid down her body again, finding the juncture of her legs, cupping and stroking the center of her need.

"Troy, I don't care what you look like now. I have to turn around and hold you, kiss you."

"Stay," he warned, his voice turning harsh and husky.

She couldn't obey. She had to reach for him.

"No!"

Chapter Nine

The spell snapped. Troy pulled away from her, leaving her gasping and swaying on her feet. She would have fallen if she hadn't reached out and caught herself against the rough trunk of a tree.

She stared after him, seeing his retreating figure clouded by the whirlwind of pine needles and moss that had heralded his arrival. He had left her the way he had come, and she could only stand in the twilight of the grove, watching until he had disappeared in a screen of underbrush.

She found her voice then, calling after him, but she knew he wouldn't answer. He had set the rules for how they would interact, and she had dared to break those rules. Her face flushed as she looked down at her disheveled clothing. She was outside, half naked. But at least her coat helped hide her from view. Quickly she pulled herself back together.

Too shaky to stand on her own, she pressed her shoulders against the tree trunk, catching her breath and thinking about what had just happened.

Over the years she had learned to stay in control of herself, she thought as she ran shaky fingers through her hair. Even when she'd become more assertive, that ability to remain steady had stood her in good stead. But today she was too off balance for control. First, she'd succumbed to a panic attack, then she'd run after Abner Sterling and finally she had let Troy sweep her away on a tide of passion. Back to a time that never was but should have been.

She stayed in the grove, trying to get herself together, physically and emotionally. She laughed when she found her purse strap was still slung over one shoulder—a testimony to a woman's ability to hang on to her pocketbook come hell or high water.

As she exhaled a deep, steadying breath, her eyes probed the shadows under the trees. Could she figure out where Troy had gone? She took a step forward, then stopped.

Now that he was no longer with her, the grove gave her the creeps. It was dark and shadowy, the perfect place for an ambush if someone wanted to come after her. But it was more than that. If she believed in bad vibes, then this place had them.

Quickly she started back toward the house. As she retraced her steps she kept a lookout for Abner Sterling. Apparently he'd been scared off by Troy's trick with the swirling debris.

Troy's trick.

Somehow he'd done those things. But how?

She was dealing with phenomena she didn't understand. Yet she desperately needed some explanation. Troy had said that people were afraid to come to this place. Had he set up machinery to make it seem like it was haunted? Did he have audio speakers and fans spread out under the trees? That would be a way to do it. She couldn't think of any other scenario.

Unless…

A small shiver traveled over her skin as she recalled the swirling matter from the forest floor. She wasn't a fanciful thinker but now she couldn't help wondering if Troy had developed some kind of supernatural powers. The idea was crazy. She never would have considered something so off the wall. But it fit so well. The way he appeared and disappeared, the way he knew what was going on.

"The Shadow knows," she murmured, remembering the old radio show her mother had listened to on tape. In the serial Lamont Cranston had traveled to the Orient where he'd acquired the ability to "cloud men's minds."

She laughed at the phrase. Probably that meant hypnosis or some other unspecified mind-control technique. Actually, there was an Alec Baldwin movie based on the old shows. Bree had rented it for her mom, and she remembered watching the parade of supernatural plot twists with a jaded eye. Now she was thinking about them in a different light.

Troy was doing things she couldn't explain in any conventional terms. Appearing and disappearing, making himself invisible, calling up a whirlwind of debris under the trees. At least it had seemed as though he'd done that. Unless she considered the possibility of some freakish weather conditions.

So, was he using hypnosis on her—and everyone else around here? Take that first night in the tunnel, when he'd disappeared and she'd crossed to the far side of the open pit, looking for him. She'd come to a rockfall and she'd had no idea where he'd escaped. But suppose he'd been there all along and he'd made it impossible for her to see him? Or suppose he'd only made the pile of rocks seem real? That was another possibility.

She dragged in a breath and let it out in a rush. If he

was using hypnotic tricks, he was manipulating her. Manipulating her perceptions and her emotions. And not simply because he wanted to make love to her. He was up to something, and she didn't know what. Now, more than ever, she needed to have a straight conversation with him. But she knew that conversation would be at his convenience. Maybe next time he'd climb down the wall of the building and let himself into her room like Dracula. She snorted. He'd been a mountain climber. Maybe he could do it. Meanwhile, she was going to get the help she needed from the Light Street Detective Agency.

THE PERSON who had been following Bree's progress since she'd stepped out of the grove crouched behind a large clump of huckleberry bushes, the compact foliage working as an excellent screen.

The watcher kept a sharp focus on the woman as she stood for a moment staring out to sea, the wind off the ocean blowing back her long blond hair in a golden curtain. Too bad she was such a pretty little thing. Too bad she'd brought herself to Ravencrest.

A few minutes ago she'd come out of that grove of trees. The grove, of all places she could have wandered on this godforsaken estate.

What was she doing nosing around in there? She'd been under the trees a long time. Plenty of time to find—

The watcher canceled the thought, unwilling to deal with the unthinkable. She hadn't found it! She couldn't have found it.

But they'd better be prepared, if the worst had happened. And they'd better not let her talk to anyone else about what she'd seen and heard here.

WITH RENEWED PURPOSE, Bree marched back across the headlands into the garden and then into the house.

After that, it took another twenty minutes to locate Nola. She found the woman sitting behind the desk in a small room on the first floor that was set up as an office. Nola's face was slightly flushed. Had she spoken to her husband?

Bree dragged her gaze from the woman and eyed the communications equipment with a mixture of thanksgiving and disappointment. There was a phone in here—the only one she'd seen in the whole damn house. And a computer sitting on the desk el. If she could come back later and use the machine, she could send an e-mail to the Light Street Detective Agency. But she'd have to be alone for that.

But she might not need e-mail. She might be able to solve her immediate problems here and now. Right in front of Nola.

The woman made her wait for several seconds while she finished writing on a sheet of paper on the desk, giving Bree more time to wonder if Abner had talked to his wife about the incident outside.

After carefully turning her work facedown on the blotter, Nola looked up questioningly at Bree. "Can I help you?" she asked, her voice calm and controlled.

"My car won't start. I was wondering who you'd recommend from town to come fix it."

"Nobody is going to come out here."

"Why not?"

"They don't like this place. There are stories about things that have happened here."

"Like what?"

"I already told you about the woman who went over the cliff and her husband who haunts the house and grounds."

In spite of her earlier resolve, Bree felt a wave of cold flow over her skin, then got control of herself again. "That was years ago."

"The folks around here have long memories."

"Well, can I use the phone? Maybe I can get somebody to change their policy."

Nola pushed back her chair and dug a phone book out of a bottom desk drawer. "Be my guest," she said as she handed over the book.

Bree sat and began going through the listings of repair shops. It wasn't long, since the nearest town, Fort Bragg, had only about six thousand people.

Quickly she found out that Nola was correct. Mechanics seemed willing to drive out of town to look at a disabled car—until they found out the work would be done at Ravencrest.

She glanced up from the last call to find Nola's gaze fixed on her. "I told you you were wasting your time," she murmured.

"Well, there are some things I forgot to bring with me from home. Would it be possible for me to borrow one of the cars here and go into town?"

Nola pulled a long face. "I'm sorry, that isn't possible. Apparently Mr. London had some trouble with his car insurance. Someone who wasn't on the policy was driving one of his vehicles and had an accident. So he was warned that his insurance would be canceled, if there was another accident with an unauthorized driver."

"I see," Bree said, keeping her voice even.

"If you need anything, give your shopping list to Graves, and he'll take care of it on his next trip into town."

"Does he like to buy tampons?" Bree snapped.

"Probably not. But he'll do it, if you need them. Or you can borrow some from me if it's an emergency."

"I don't need them right now. I was just giving an example," Bree muttered, wondering if she could steal a car and make her getaway with Dinah in tow. But first she'd have to find the keys and match them to a vehicle.

"I don't like it any more than you do," Nola muttered, and for a moment Bree thought she was going to say something more. Then her expression closed up again.

"Well, I'll make a list of what I need," Bree said, then hesitated. She wanted to ask why there was only one phone in this huge house, but no doubt she wouldn't get a straight answer.

As she left the room she debated what to do next, then decided she should check on Dinah.

Mrs. Martindale was in the kitchen getting ready for dinner. When Bree asked about the little girl, the house-keeper directed her down a short hall to a cozy sitting room that was probably the servant's lounge. It was out-fitted with a comfortable couch and chair, both facing a large television set.

Dinah was on the sofa eating pretzels from a bowl and watching a Disney video.

She looked up as Bree came in.

"Can I turn off your program for a minute?" Bree asked.

"For a minute," the child answered, making it clear that she didn't really want to be interrupted.

Bree clicked the stop button on the VCR, then sat on the couch. "I know you like to watch videos, but we could play a game instead."

"I want to find out how Cinderella comes out."

"You haven't seen it before?"

"No. Mrs. Martindale just got it out. She keeps new ones around for a surprise."

Bree thought about keeping the child company. She wanted to spend more time with Dinah but she wasn't going to be pushy about it. So she said, "You watch the movie. I'll see you at dinner, then."

"Okay."

Bree clicked the video on again, then started back toward her room, thinking she might as well get some rest. As she made her way down the hall she heard voices and stopped. Mrs. Martindale was talking to someone, her tone sharper than Bree had heard it before. She stopped in the hall, aware that she was eavesdropping, yet willing to use any means she could to find out about the situation at Ravencrest.

"What's wrong with you? This isn't a good time," the housekeeper was saying.

"Then when do you suggest I come back, if you don't mind my asking?"

Bree recognized the other speaker. It was Foster Graves, the spooky handyman.

"I suggest you come back later," Mrs. Martindale said firmly. "When I'm not...cooking dinner."

After a space of several seconds there was a grudging, "Okay."

Bree waited a few beats to make sure the conversation was finished, then stepped briskly down the hall and entered the kitchen again. "Problems?" she asked as she took in Mrs. Martindale's slightly flushed face.

"That was Graves," she said.

"Yes, I heard him."

The housekeeper looked exasperated. "I asked him two days ago to check the drain in the kitchen sink. It's sluggish. So he shows up now to fix it. When I explained to him it wasn't a good time, he got that stubborn look that makes me so annoyed.''

Bree nodded. So Graves was stubborn. She might have added that the man gave her the creeps. But she didn't know his relationship with the housekeeper. Their conversation hadn't exactly sounded friendly, but she wasn't going to make any assumptions.

''I'll be in my room if you need me,'' Bree said.

''Yes. Fine.''

She'd simply been going to get some rest. But she felt a strange sense of urgency as she started back to her quarters. By the time she reached the upstairs hall, she was running. Maybe…maybe Troy would be there.

With a feeling of anticipation, she threw open the door. But the room was empty. She felt her shoulders sag as she stepped through the door.

She leaned back against the wall and took several deep breaths. She had a right to be keyed up after the events of the day. Relaxing before dinner was an excellent idea.

First she crossed to the bathroom and used the facilities. Then she turned to the sink and began to wash her hands. She was just drying them when a sound stopped her. At first she only felt it as a vibration under her feet. The vibration grew, swelled, resolved itself into the same strange drumming she'd heard in the grove. It was followed by the unexpected sound of voices in the bedroom.

''What are you doing?'' she heard a man's voice say.

It was Troy! Somehow she'd expected to find him here.

She started to open the bathroom door, then was stopped by another speaker. ''Where did you come from?'' a man asked, his voice made high and thin by fear so that she had no idea who it was.

''That's not important. Answer my question.''

She heard rapid footsteps then, followed by a dull, thudding noise like a hard object hitting flesh and bone—followed by what sounded like broken glass raining onto the floor.

She'd been frozen in place. Now she realized that Troy was in trouble.

There was no thought for her own safety. She had to help him. Looking wildly around for a weapon, she picked up the plaster statue of a water nymph from the shelf over the toilet tank and burst through the door into her room.

It was empty.

She blinked, trying to take in what she was—or wasn't—seeing as she stood there, her breath coming in gasps. The room was just as she'd left it. No one was here.

But she'd heard the beating of the drum and what sounded like a malicious assault.

The vibrations were almost below the limit of human awareness now. But she still felt them.

Quickly she crossed to the closet and pulled the door open, but no one was there, either.

"Troy?" she called as she'd done so many times before.

There was no reply, but the thrumming surged, making the air around her vibrate. It was like the whirlwind in the woods, only more subtle. And there was nothing to see. She could only feel the currents of air pulsing around her.

She'd come tearing in here in an agony of fear, prepared to rescue Troy. Now the stirring of the atmosphere around her turned soft and gentle, soothing the panic away. It calmed her down, convinced her that everything was all right once again. She closed her eyes, thinking that the sensation was almost like the caress of a hand on her hair, on her cheek, on her lips. Troy's caress. Because it felt so much as though he was really here.

Far, far in the background she heard music. Once again Rod Stewart was singing "Tonight's the Night."

"What's tonight? Are you finally going to make love to me?" she murmured, her voice dreamy as she swayed to the beat of the ballad.

The words simply tumbled out of her mouth. Her eyes blinked open and she found herself standing in an empty room. Technically empty. But still it was alive with elements that were real—elements just beyond the threshold of time and space.

The currents of air seemed to wrap themselves more tightly around her, holding her in an embrace that was both tender and sensual.

"Stay with me. Let me see you," she pleaded.

He didn't show himself. But he stayed for long minutes. And then, all at once, it was over. She was alone in her room.

Troy had been here. He hadn't let her see him and he hadn't spoken. But he'd held her, touched her, comforted her, somehow using the special powers he'd acquired. Now he was gone.

She didn't realize he'd been holding her up until she found that her legs wouldn't support her weight. She swayed on her feet, tottered to the overstuffed chair and collapsed in a heap, her head thrown back and her legs sprawled out in front of her.

She was still drifting, still muzzy-headed. Troy had done that to her. Clouded her mind, she thought with a little giggle.

Gradually, over a span of several minutes, the otherworldly sensations subsided and she came back to herself. As she did, she began to wonder what had happened. The events might have been triggered by hypnosis or something chemical, some type of hallucinogen. She recalled hearing about a similar thing in a case at the agency. Whatever the cause, the pattern of events was significant.

Deliberately, she went back to the scenes she'd overheard from the other side of the bathroom door.

It had started with a frightening incident: Troy asking a question then getting ambushed.

She swallowed the sick feeling that had suddenly risen in her throat. She'd asked Troy what had happened to him and he'd said he didn't remember. Maybe the memory had come back to him and he'd chosen this way to answer her question. Or maybe it was a fantasy he was showing her.

If he was only showing her a fantasy, why frighten her? So he would have an excuse to comfort her afterward? That hardly seemed like something he would do. At least, not the old Troy London. The new Troy was mysterious and secretive and devious. He'd manipulated her before. Why not again? Maybe he wanted to frighten her, so she'd take Dinah and leave the estate as he'd asked her to do.

There was no way to be sure what had happened. But it was impossible not to feel as though someone—maybe Troy—was playing with her mind.

Pushing herself up, she stiffened her knees, then crossed to the bathroom again, where she splashed water on her face before taking several sips.

Feeling she could think better, she turned back to the bedroom, searching it in a new light, bringing back each detail of the attack, examining each in isolation.

The episode had ended with glass breaking.

She focused on that detail, then ran to the light switch and turned on the overhead fixture as well as all the lamps. If someone had broken a bottle or a vase in here, they had obviously cleaned it up. But had they gotten all the glass?

At first she saw nothing when she started to search along the baseboards. Then her heart leaped into her windpipe when she saw the tiny speck glittering in the crack where the floor met the wall. There were more tiny pieces that would have been easy to miss if she hadn't been searching for them, and a larger one—a quarter of an inch long, sticking upright.

When she reached to pick it up, a sharp edge dug itself into her finger and she made a small sound as blood welled from the injury. Cupping her palm around the dripping finger, she hurried to the bathroom, grabbed a tissue and pulled out the piece of glass. Then she washed off the finger and put on a bandage from her medicine kit.

Back in her bedroom, she sat in the chair and looked around the room once more. It could be that something totally unrelated to Troy had happened here. Something from long ago. Such as the ghost. But she didn't think so.

The speculation made her chest tighten. She hated to think that Troy had been attacked in this bedroom where she was sleeping. But it might be one of the reasons he kept coming here. Even when he'd lost his conscious memory of the incident, he might have remembered it on some level.

Suppose he'd been hit on the head and that had created strange side effects—such as awakening psychic powers. Or suppose he already had some kind of powers and the blow to the head had somehow sharpened them. And now he was calling forth those arcane abilities while he traveled silently around the estate, using the secret passages he and Helen had discovered when they were children.

She sighed. All of that was simply speculation. She really didn't know what had happened—or how he was creating the special effects that seemed to accompany her contact with him.

And then there was an even more important question: who had hurt him? She'd come here thinking the Sterlings were the prime candidates. Perhaps they were working with Graves and he was directing the show.

There was one more point she had to consider. Strange things had been happening since she'd arrived here and she'd basically accepted them all at face value. Did that mean she should be calling her own sanity into question? Abner Sterling had called this place an insane asylum. Maybe all you had to do was live in this house to go insane.

Chapter Ten

Resolutely, Bree regained her composure. When she felt she was equipped to come in contact with the people on the estate, she went down to the kitchen and found Mrs. Martindale preparing dinner.

"I've been thinking about Dinah's meals being served in the schoolroom. She's there so much. Is there somewhere else she and I could have dinner?" Bree asked.

Mrs. Martindale considered the question. "We have lots of rooms that aren't used much. There's a sunporch near her bedroom. Would that do?"

"I think so." She cleared her throat. "Uh, can I help you get dinner ready?"

"Oh, no, dear. That's not your job. I'm almost finished. You could help me fill plates for you and the little girl, though. She already went up to her room."

Bree helped transfer peas and carrots, pieces of roast chicken and parsley potatoes to dinner plates, then cleared her throat. The last time she'd ask the housekeeper questions, the answers hadn't been much help. Now she felt she had to try again.

"Can I ask you something?" she murmured.

"Certainly."

"When Ms. London hired me, she said that Mr. London's wife had died. Do you know how it happened?"

The housekeeper paused in the act of setting a slice of whole wheat bread on one of the plates. "Why do you want to know that?"

"Well, Dinah seems so shy. I'd like to…draw her out but I don't want to say the wrong thing."

"Yes. I understand." The woman sighed. "Mrs. London died in an automobile accident."

"Was she in the car alone?"

"Oh, no. Mr. London was driving."

Bree's mouth had gone dry. Troy had told her that Grace was driving the car. "*He* was driving?"

"Why, yes. It was a terrible burden for him. He became quite distraught. I understand that's what led to his nervous breakdown."

"Oh" was all Bree could manage.

"A real tragedy," the housekeeper was saying. "He was such a young, vital man."

"Yes." Bree's head was spinning. Troy had lied to her. Or maybe in his mind, that was what he thought had happened because he couldn't deal with the reality. Or maybe the housekeeper had her facts wrong.

She watched the woman cut slices of chocolate cake and set them on smaller plates, then pour drinks. Milk for Dinah and a glass of iced tea for Bree, who added lemon and sugar.

Since Mrs. Martindale seemed to be in a talkative mood, Bree asked the jackpot question, "Uh, where *is* Mr. London?"

The housekeeper hesitated for a moment. "We don't know." She lowered her voice. "He's disappeared, and we've been so worried."

"Then why did Mrs. Sterling tell me he was locked in his room? Why do I see you carrying food up there?"

"I think Mrs. Sterling didn't want you to worry about the situation. And about the food—sometimes it's been eaten when I go back to collect the tray. So I guess he has some way of slipping in and out of his room when he wants to." She laughed. "Or Abner Sterling is getting in there and stuffing himself."

Bree mulled that over. "But if Mr. London is at large on the estate, isn't that dangerous?"

"He's never been a danger to anyone else as far as I know," the housekeeper murmured.

That contradicted what Nola had told her, Bree thought as she pressed on. "But isn't he at risk? I mean, a risk to himself," she asked, struggling to keep her voice steady. "If he's sick, you can't just leave him wandering around."

"What choice do we have? He knows this place like the back of his hand. If he doesn't want to be found, he won't be. And don't ask me to set a trap in his room. I had Graves sitting up there for two days a few weeks ago, and Mr. London just stayed away."

Bree was shocked by the information the housekeeper had revealed. It sounded as though Mrs. Martindale was starting to trust her. But when Bree saw the woman watch her speculatively, she only gave a tight nod.

"We'd better take the dinner up before it gets cold," she said.

"Yes."

They both carried covered trays up the back stairs and the older woman led the way to the sunporch. It was a very pretty place to eat, with bright peach-and-yellow cushions on wicker furniture. Wide glass windows gave a panoramic view of the headlands and the ocean. After her conversation with Troy about Grace's spending habits, Bree saw the room a little differently than she might have earlier. Before, it might have just looked pretty. Now she could see that a lot of money had gone into decorating it.

Unbidden, a terrible thought leaped into her mind. What if Troy had killed his wife because she was bleeding him dry with her overblown spending? As soon as the idea surfaced, she was horrified that she could even have thought it.

Tensely she waited for Mrs. Martindale to leave the room, thinking she was no closer to the truth than before she'd asked her questions. It was like being at a trial where each witness told a different story and there was no way to know who was lying. Well, not yet, anyway, Bree thought as she hurried down the hall. As she stepped into Dinah's room, she stopped and looked around, and the same thoughts she'd had earlier surfaced again. The bedroom was an expensively created dream room for a little girl, decorated in pink and white with lots of ruffles and a three-tier-high shelf along one wall crammed with toys and books. The whole package had to have cost more than a luxury car.

Stop questioning the details of his marriage, Bree ordered herself as she focused on Dinah who was sitting on her bed, propped up against a raft of pillows. A picture book was open on her lap, but instead of looking at the pages, she was staring across the room toward the flowered wallpaper, her gaze unfocused as though she were lost in a dreamworld of her own.

''Dinah, dinner's ready,'' Bree said brightly.

The girl's attention snapped to the doorway. She looked embarrassed, as though she'd been caught doing something she shouldn't.

Bree kept her own expression friendly. "And I have a nice surprise. We're going to eat on the sunporch."

The child nodded, set her book aside and scrambled off the bed, where she paused to push her feet into fuzzy bedroom slippers, then grabbed Alice.

In the sunroom, she set her kitten beside her on the chair, then made a face when Bree uncovered the trays. "I hate peas and carrots."

"Me, too. Let's not eat them!"

The child looked startled. "You're saying we don't have to eat everything?"

"That's what I'm saying." Grinning, Bree pulled out her chair and sat.

"And I can still have chocolate cake for dessert?" Dinah clarified.

"Absolutely."

A smile flickered on the child's face as she took her seat.

"And you can pick up your pieces of chicken, if you want. That's what I like to do." Demonstrating, she grabbed a chicken leg and took a bite.

Dinah followed suit, then asked, "Where did you live when you were a little girl?"

"In Greensboro, North Carolina. My mom was a schoolteacher."

"Like you."

"Yes."

"What about your daddy?"

"He…left us when I was very small. I don't really remember much about him."

"Oh. Do you still live with your mom?" Dinah asked.

"She died a few years ago."

"And that made you sad."

"Of course."

"My mom died," Dinah murmured.

How did she die? Bree wanted desperately to ask, but she didn't so as not to bring back painful memories. Instead she said, "I know. That must have been so hard on you—especially if your daddy was very sad and he didn't want to spend a lot of time with you."

Dinah shifted in her seat. "Who told you about that?"

Bree thought for a moment about what she ought to say. Up till now she'd been cautious about asking Dinah too many probing questions, because their relationship was new and she didn't want to come across as prying. But now it felt right to try to get some information. Still, there was another consideration. Was there any chance that someone could be listening to their conversation? She decided to assume that speaking freely was all right in this room, since it wasn't a place that anyone regularly frequented. If somebody had gone to the trouble of bugging it, then the whole house would be bugged.

"Your aunt Helen," she finally answered. "She and I met when we were in college at Chapel Hill. And we became very good friends."

"I haven't seen Aunt Helen for a long time."

"Neither have I, because she's out of the country. But she called me and said she was worried about you and your daddy. She wanted me to find out how you were doing."

Dinah nodded gravely, then said in a low voice, "Daddy said I could trust you. But I wasn't sure it really was Daddy."

Bree's head jerked up. "He talked to you—but you're not sure it's him?"

The child averted her face. "I never see him or touch him. But sometimes we have conversations. Then I don't know if it was a dream."

"You talk to him at night?"

"Yes. When it's dark."

Bree dragged in a breath and let it out slowly. "Thank you for telling me," she said.

"I couldn't tell anyone else."

"Did your daddy say why he's…hiding?"

"No." Dinah's voice quavered.

Bree pushed back her chair, came around the table and knelt beside the girl's seat. Earlier she'd been shocked by Mrs. Martindale's revelation and was still hoping the part about Troy's nervous breakdown wasn't true. Maybe he had good reasons for hiding out. She didn't know what to believe anymore.

But she was pretty sure what it must be like for Dinah to catch snatches of the adults' conversation and worry and wonder.

Reaching out, she gathered her close. Dinah held herself stiffly and Bree fought a wave of disappointment. Then the child relaxed against her. Bree shifted her hold, picked Dinah up and moved to one of the wicker chairs, where she sat and cradled the girl on her lap, feeling her narrow shoulders begin to shake.

Feeling as if a barrier had fallen, Bree held her, rocked her, stroked her, while she cried softly the way she hadn't been able to do out in the garden a few days ago. Finally the tears stopped and Bree found a tissue in her pants' pocket.

Dinah blew her nose. Still with her head tipped downward, she whispered, "At night, I'm scared. So sometimes I pretend that Daddy's with me."

"I understand.

"And sometimes during the day, too," she admitted. "Nobody here is nice—except Mrs. Martindale. And sometimes she's in a bad mood, too."

"Well, I hope I'm nice."

"You are! I didn't mean you."

Bree hesitated for a moment then said, "We shouldn't tell anyone we talked about your aunt Helen or your daddy. If he's hiding out, then we should keep it a secret."

"I tried to tell Mrs. Martindale once, but it made her be in a bad mood."

"All the more reason not to tell anyone—even her. Okay?"

The girl nodded vigorously. "Yes."

Bree softened her voice. "Were you pretending that first time you saw me in the front hall? When you told Mrs. Sterling that your daddy had said I was coming."

Dinah looked down. "Yes," she whispered. "Are you mad at me?"

"Of course not. I understand." She put a gentle finger on the girl's chin and raised her head. "Let's eat some more of our dinner and our chocolate cake. Then I can read you a story, if you'd like."

Again the girl nodded. But as she ate her cake, Bree sensed that she was restless.

"Did you want to ask me a question?" she asked.

Dinah pressed her lips together, then blurted, "Do you think my daddy loves me?"

"Of course he does!"

"Then why won't he let me see him?"

Bree considered several possible answers. None of them seemed quite right, so she finally said, "I guess he has his reasons. I guess we'll find out when he's ready to tell us."

That seemed to satisfy Dinah, who took another bite of cake.

"Do you have a favorite book?" Bree asked when they were almost finished with dessert.

"Daddy got me Harry Potter. We were reading it—until he stopped being here during the day."

"I love Harry Potter. I'd love to finish reading it to you."

"That means you're going to be here a long time."

"Yes."

Bree spent the rest of the evening with Dinah, even overseeing her bath and getting her ready for bed.

By the time she'd tucked the child in, she was tired—but pleased. She'd worked hard at making friends with the girl, and it looked as though her efforts were paying off. She wanted to help Dinah, but she was also thinking that she might get some vital information from the girl—information Dinah might not even know she possessed.

Back in her room, she lay down with her clothing on since she was planning to get up later. Outside she could hear the waves crashing against the rocks at the bottom of the cliffs. But from time to time she was aware of creaking noises that made her wonder if someone was out in the hall.

In the darkened room she dozed, floating on a current of fatigue. The texture of her unconsciousness changed subtly and a hand touched her hair. And warm breath flirted with her ear.

"Thank you," Troy murmured.

"For what?" she asked, her voice sleepy, her eyes closed. In some part of her mind she was thinking that after that conversation with Mrs. Martindale, perhaps she should be afraid of him. But he'd never hurt her. And he'd had plenty of chances.

"Thank you for making friends with Dinah," he answered. "You're good for her. She needs…someone who cares about her."

"I do!"

He kissed the tender line where her hair met her cheek and she drifted, enjoying the sensations.

"Mrs. Martindale is okay, but I don't trust her," he said.

"Why not?" she asked, holding her breath, waiting for him to give her some reason to discount the housekeeper's disturbing story.

"Sometimes I think I know why. Other times…it's just a feeling."

She sighed. She wanted to ask him about the car accident. Perhaps she didn't because she was afraid to hear the answer. She might have reached to turn on the bedside light, but she remembered what had happened before when she'd tried to get a good look at him. He'd simply vanished. And she didn't want that now. So she lay quietly in bed, enjoying the feeling of being close to him.

Still, she couldn't simply remain passive. "Troy," she murmured, "something bad happened in this room. I…heard it when I was in the bathroom. Then I came bursting through the door and nobody was here. And I decided that I wasn't really hearing something that had just happened. Instead it was something that took place earlier."

When he didn't respond, she went on. "Did you make me hear that? Did you remember being attacked and picked that way to tell me about it? Do you have… special powers?" she said, wondering if he'd admit it to her.

"Special powers? What do you mean?"

"You can do things—like that trick in the grove of

making the pine needles and stuff swirl. How did you do that?''

"I don't know. I just did it."

She felt a surge of victory. He'd admitted that much to her, even if he wasn't going to tell her how he'd accomplished the feat.

Encouraged, she went back to her previous topic. "Then this afternoon you brought me the sound images of a confrontation here."

"Yes."

"How did you do it?"

"It's like the pine needles. I just do it."

"Who was here with you?"

"I don't know. I can't see it. I can only hear it."

"Thank you for telling me. It makes me feel closer to you."

His voice turned urgent as he said, "If you want to do something for me, get Dinah out of here."

He'd said that before, which meant it must be weighing on his mind.

"What about you?"

"It's too late for me."

"No!" Her eyes snapped open and she reached out a hand to grab him. But in the shaft of moonlight coming from the edge of the billowing curtains, she could see she was alone.

Had Troy come to her, or had she just imagined the whole conversation?

On the floor below, a grandfather clock struck midnight, reminding her of the decision she'd made earlier.

Troy had told her to get out of here and to take Dinah. But it was clear she wasn't going to do it without help.

Hoping it was late enough to make an assault on the

office, she pulled on slippers and stepped into the hall, waiting for her eyes to adjust to the darkness.

It was still as death as she headed for the stairs, praying that she didn't run into Graves the way she had that first afternoon when she'd been going to investigate Troy's room.

On the steps, she trod lightly, but every time one of the old risers squeaked, she froze. Finally, she made it to the main floor and breathed out a little sigh.

Feeling like a thief in the night, she tiptoed toward the kitchen and retrieved the flashlight from the cabinet where Mrs. Martindale kept it.

She was about to step into the hall again when the sound of voices made her freeze in her tracks.

It was Nola and Abner, heading toward her, just around a bend in the hallway.

She had only seconds to find a hiding place or to come up with an explanation for her presence down here.

She chose stealth. Slipping behind the kitchen door, she pressed her shoulders against the wall.

Abner came clomping down the passageway. Nola's quick, nervous little steps accompanied him. They were speaking in harsh whispers, but their voices carried easily to Bree's hiding place.

Lord, what if they were coming to the kitchen? She froze, trying to blend into the walls, knowing that if she moved, they would discover her.

She waited for the pounding of her heart to give her away. It sounded to her as loud as the drumming noise she'd heard in the grove of trees.

Their steps slowed and she felt her throat close. Then they made their way past the doorway and she eased out the breath she'd been holding.

Nola began to speak. "You know what I wish? I wish

Helen had never invited us here. If I'd known she was going to give us all those damn directions about what we could and couldn't say, I would have told her to shove it.''

''You had a better suggestion?'' Abner asked. ''We were flat broke and the invitation was a godsend.''

Bree didn't hear her answer. She was still focused on the woman's previous statement. Had she heard that right? Helen had invited them?

Surely that must be a mistake. Helen had told her that the Sterlings were distant cousins down on their luck and that Troy had allowed them to move in—over her veto. She'd said she was worried about what the Sterlings might have done since arriving because Troy wasn't paying enough attention to the world around him.

While Bree was trying to make sense out of that, Nola spoke again.

''You've got to find him!''

''Don't you think I've tried?''

''He's got the run of the estate. But I never see him.''

''Nobody sees him,'' Abner snapped. ''Except the kid. And two to one, she's lying.''

They were talking about Troy. And it sounded as if they had the same opinion as Mrs. Martindale.

Bree focused in on the conversation again in time to hear Nola say, ''But he does things. Like that music this afternoon in his room.''

''The schoolteacher could be lying. She could have turned it on.''

''Maybe. But I'm sure she wasn't in our bedroom this morning. I found my calcium pills emptied into the trash can.''

''The bottle could have fallen in.''

''No. The empty bottle was on the sink.''

Abner sighed. "You don't know it was him. The old lady could have done it by accident and might not want to own up to it. Or maybe it was Graves, trying to spook you. He's spooky enough even when he's not up to mischief. It could be him, trying to make us think that London is up to no good—when he's dead."

Dead! Bree felt an icy shiver travel down her spine.

"You don't know if he's dead. You haven't found any evidence. There's more evidence that he's alive."

"I say he's dead, and it's his ghost haunting us—for revenge. There's a tradition of ghosts in this damn place."

Bree pressed a hand to her mouth to keep from making a sound, and Nola said something she couldn't catch.

"I didn't think you believed in ghosts," Abner answered.

"I didn't. Until I came here. But we're not going to settle anything by arguing about it," Nola muttered. "I want to get away from this place. I'm tired of telling lies so nobody will question why we're staying here."

"Yeah, me, too. But this is a lot more comfortable than living out of the back of a van."

Nola sighed.

"Just hang in there for a little while longer until I can work some kind of deal," Abner said, his voice more gentle.

"You and your deals. That's how we always get into trouble."

"This time is different. The money is going to start rolling in. You'll see."

"Right."

Sliding her gaze around the corner of the doorway, Bree watched the couple head toward the office.

Lord, they sounded as though they were in pretty bad

shape. Frightened and paranoid. She'd assumed that they were in charge of things here, but it sounded as if they were captives of circumstances.

And what about Troy? Mrs. Martindale said he was on the loose, hiding out around the estate. Abner thought he was dead.

But he wasn't dead. She'd talked to him and felt his touch. He'd felt warm and alive. Yet the encounters had all been so strange. And although Dinah had talked to him, she couldn't remember seeing him.

Her heart blocked her windpipe and she ordered herself to get a grip. From the conversation, it sounded as though the Sterlings had had some frightening experiences since Troy had disappeared. Bree had rationalized her own strange encounters with him by telling herself that Troy had unexplained powers he could use to keep himself hidden and to create special effects.

Apparently the Sterlings were making different assumptions.

Maybe reading that book in the library had gotten Nola started on the ghost theme.

Bree rubbed her hands over her arms, trying to wipe away the cold, clammy feeling that had suddenly enveloped her.

She wanted to sprint back to the relative safety of her room but she couldn't do it yet. At the moment she was trapped in the kitchen. If she stepped into the hall, the Sterlings might come back this way and spot her.

So she stood where she was, pressing her shoulder to the wall and shifting her weight from one foot to the other, hoping Mrs. Martindale didn't decide to come down here in the middle of the night.

It seemed like a thousand endless years before she heard a door open, heard footsteps again. This time the

Sterlings were silent as they made their way down the hall to the stairs.

Bree waited another five minutes after she'd heard them climb the steps. When she couldn't stand still another minute, she tiptoed quietly down the hall to the office.

She was prepared to use her lock pick. But that wasn't necessary.

Inside she switched on the flashlight. But she soon found out that merely getting inside the office had done her little good. There was some kind of night lock on the phone, so she couldn't lift the receiver. Maybe she could wrench it off but she was pretty sure she couldn't get it back on.

It entered her mind that maybe she should let them think the ghost had done it. The idea of the prank made her grin, until a more sobering thought struck her. The Sterlings had sounded pretty stressed out. Maybe more ghostly shenanigans would push them over the edge. She didn't want to find out what would happen in that case.

Since the phone was useless to her, she beamed the flashlight on the computer.

It had been turned off for the night, and she'd have to reboot. Setting the flashlight down on the desk, she flipped the power switch. The machine started through its opening routine—then stopped.

"Enter password."

Oh, great. Just what she needed. Of course she didn't know the password. She made several sensible tries. Ravencrest. Helen. Dinah. The child's birthday. None of them worked.

Another worry began to nag at her. Was there some kind of alarm attached to the machine that would sound after a certain number of wrong guesses?

She stopped, knowing she had to take a different approach. Maybe the password was written down.

She pulled out the middle desk drawer and felt around on the underside, hoping to find a piece of paper taped to the thin wood panel.

There was no paper, but she found something else—a small, flat piece of metal that felt like a key.

It was taped securely in place and she had to work at it with her fingernails. Finally it came free, and she had just picked up the flashlight to look at it when the doorknob turned and the door burst open.

Chapter Eleven

Bree clutched the little key in her palm as she whirled to face the door, pushing the drawer partly closed with her hip.

She thought she'd be confronting Nola or Abner again. Instead Mrs. Martindale stood in the doorway.

"Oh, my," she said. "I didn't expect to find you here."

"I…" Bree mentally scrambled for something to say. Finally she settled on a version of the truth. Falling back on her ditz-brained persona, she fluttered her hands and said, "Ravencrest makes me so nervous. And I'm so homesick. I was hoping to talk to one of my friends, but the phone is locked up so I thought maybe I could send some e-mail. But I don't know the password."

Mrs. Martindale's face twisted. "Yes, Nola doesn't want unauthorized phone or computer use. She says it's an economy measure."

"Why? Is there a financial problem here?"

The housekeeper sniffed. "You'll have to ask her about that."

As the woman spoke Bree casually slipped her hand into her pocket, leaving the key tucked out of sight.

After a silent debate she said, "I'd appreciate if you

didn't tell Mrs. Sterling I was in the office. I don't want to get on her bad side.''

Mrs. Martindale made a tsking sound. ''I understand. She can be quite trying.''

''How did she happen to be in charge here?'' Bree asked.

''She's a relative of the Londons.''

''Oh, yes,'' she responded once more.

The conversation had wound down, but the housekeeper remained standing in the doorway and Bree got the definite impression that she wasn't going to be left alone in the office. Leaning back, she closed the drawer the rest of the way with her hip.

''I see you borrowed the flashlight again,'' Mrs. Martindale said. ''If you're finished with it, I'd like to have it back.''

''Of course. I, uh, didn't want to bother anyone by turning on the light in here.'' She knew the excuse was lame, but it was all she could think of.

''Yes. There was only a little light coming from under the door. But I felt like I should investigate. It could have been a fire,'' the housekeeper responded as she crossed the room and turned off the computer.

As Bree moved toward the door Mrs. Martindale backed up. In the hall, Bree handed over the flashlight.

She still felt uncomfortable, but there was nothing she could do about that. And she had the feeling that the less she said about her visit to the office, the better.

Yet questions were still buzzing in her mind.

''I was wondering something about Helen London,'' she said.

''Yes?''

''Was it Ms. London who invited the Sterlings to come here?''

"Certainly not! She didn't know a thing about it."

"How do you know?"

"I wrote her a letter, telling her what was happening. And she wrote me back."

"Oh. Yes," she murmured, wishing that the woman's answers would match the Sterlings'.

Figuring she was going to arouse suspicion if she kept probing, Bree took her leave of the housekeeper and made her way to the back stairs, feeling the woman watch her progress.

Still, it looked as if she'd gotten off easy, as long as Mrs. Martindale kept her word and didn't blab to Nola.

Back in her room she shut and locked the door, leaning back against the stout wooden barrier as she exhaled a long breath. It made her feel safer to lock herself in. But she knew it was a false sense of security. Anyone who wanted to get to her could do so by coming down the tunnel, through the far entrance that she hadn't been able to find.

For that matter, they could spring the lock on the door—or break it down.

Unbidden, the image of a crazed Jack Nicholson in *The Shining* leaped into her mind. She'd been around eleven years old, sitting in front of the television one evening while Mom was out with her friends when *The Shining* had come on.

She'd heard about it and she'd decided to watch. Big mistake. Soon she was so frightened by the violent images on the screen that she couldn't move. It was before the era of the ubiquitous remote control and she'd been too afraid to abandon the safety of Mom's bed to turn off the set. So she'd sat there, staring at scenes that made the hair on the back of her neck feel like knives stabbing into her flesh. Then Jack Nicholson, intent on killing his wife and child, had battered through the door to their apartment with an ax and stuck his head through the opening, grinning maniacally.

The image still made her shudder. She didn't really think anyone would come after her with an ax. Probably it would be something more subtle, like Mrs. Martindale slipping poison into her tuna sandwich.

Stop it, she warned herself. Mrs. Martindale wasn't the enemy. But she wouldn't bet her life on that.

Knowing the best thing to do now was to take a hot shower and get a good night's rest, she pulled out a nightgown, took it into the bathroom and closed the door. First she turned on the water in the shower, giving it a chance to run hot. Then she took off her clothes and laid them on the sink. The key she'd found taped to the bottom of the desk drawer was still in her pocket.

Briefly she considered hiding it somewhere in the room. But her room had been searched before and could be again.

After adjusting the water, she stepped into the clawfooted tub and pulled the shower curtain that encircled it.

The hot water was like a balm to her jangled nerves. She let the spray pound on her back for a couple of minutes, then began to wash her body.

It was such an ordinary action, something she did every day. Washing herself. Yet this time her hand stopped in the act of soaping her breast, as she imagined that someone was observing her.

Her free hand clenched. She'd been thinking how easy it would be for someone to come into the room. Now her gaze shot to the shower curtain. It was translucent, and she saw a hazy image of the bathroom fixtures.

But that was all. There was no one standing in the

room. Still, just to make sure, she stuck her head around the curtain and peered out, the cold air from the room chilling her skin and making her nipples tighten.

The scene hadn't changed. Nobody was there.

With a sigh, she withdrew behind the curtain again. Then, defying her attack of nerves, she poured shampoo into her hand. Closing her eyes, she worked a lather in her hair. She was finger combing the shampoo into her scalp when she felt it again—the sensation of eyes on her.

Stop it! she ordered herself.

Water and shampoo were running down her face, and she knew she'd be making a painful mistake if she opened her eyes. As quickly as possible, she rinsed the suds out of her hair, then grabbed the plastic bottle of shampoo. It wasn't much of a weapon, but it was the best she could do. Turning her head slowly, she looked toward the shower curtain again. Once more, to her vast relief, she found no one standing beyond the flimsy barrier.

Was there a hidden camera in the bathroom? She hadn't thought to look for one in here. Maybe that had been another mistake.

In the *Baltimore Sun,* she'd read about a dirty old man who rented apartments to young women and videotaped their most intimate moments in the bedroom and bathroom. Could Graves the handyman be up to something like that?

Her enthusiasm for the shower had evaporated. With a grimace, she turned off the water, then pulled the curtain partially aside and stared at the light fixture, the window frame, the mirror on the medicine cabinet. They all looked utterly ordinary. But they would, wouldn't they?

Ready to step out of the tub, she switched her gaze downward, making sure she didn't slip as she climbed over the high side. As she focused on the bath mat, she froze, and a wave of cold swept over her, peppering her skin with goose bumps.

In the white pile of the small rug she saw the impression of two footprints.

They weren't her small ones, but two much larger prints of tennis shoes. A man's shoes, unless one of the women here wore size fourteen or fifteen—and she didn't remember Nola or Mrs. Martindale clumping around in rowboats.

She stopped in midstride, her hand clamping on the edge of the tub as she peered downward, telling herself she must be mistaken. That she had imagined the imprints.

But they remained firmly in her line of vision.

She'd been right the first time. She wasn't being watched on a video camera. Someone had been here! Someone had been out in the bedroom, then come into the bathroom, in the few minutes when she'd had her eyes closed.

Quickly her arm shot out and she grabbed the towel from the rack, wrapping it around herself like a security blanket and hiding her nakedness. For all the good that did her now.

She didn't want to leave the bathroom. But if someone had been standing right beside the shower, she wasn't safe anyway. Gingerly, she stepped around the bath mat, the cold floor hitting the soles of her feet and seeping into her bones.

After drying off in record time, she looked at the nightgown she'd laid out. It would make her feel too exposed. Instead of pulling it on, she got fresh underwear out of the suitcase she'd set on the stool in the corner and then redressed in the shirt and pants she'd been wearing.

As she dressed, she tried to talk herself out of her previous conclusion. Maybe the footprints were not what she thought. Maybe something about the steamy atmosphere in the room had brought out previous impressions on the rug.

It was a reasonable theory, she told herself. And she added more details. While she'd been in the shower, she hadn't felt the wave of cold air she should have felt if the door had been opened.

Stepping back into the bedroom, she crossed to the door and checked the lock. It was secure. So was the closet door. But so what? After the episode in the shower, the idea of staying in this room gave her the creeps. And she knew that she wasn't going to get a moment's sleep if she stayed here.

Returning to the bathroom, she did a quick job of blow drying her hair. Then she looked around the bedroom, wishing that her gun hadn't disappeared. Finally she unplugged the cut-glass lamp on the bedside table and removed the silk shade. Clutching the cylindrical base in her hand, she tiptoed to the door and listened. When she heard nothing, she cautiously turned the lock and looked out into the hall.

Torn between feeling foolish and needing to feel safe, she left the bedroom, closed the door and stood in the hall, trying to decide where to go.

An image came to her. An image of Troy's room. Nola had given her a direct order to stay away from there. Which meant getting caught disobeying instructions would put her in jeopardy.

Yet once the idea took hold, she simply couldn't dislodge it from her mind. It was almost as if Troy was talking to her inside her head, compelling her to come to him. Telling her she'd be safe in his bed.

Returning briefly to the room she'd just left, she grabbed the lock-picking kit. Then she tiptoed quietly along the hallway to the back stairs. On the landing at the top she waited for several minutes, making sure that no one else was up here walking around.

Then she hurried down the hall to Troy's room. When she tried the knob, she found the door was unlocked.

The only explanation that made sense was that Troy had opened the door for her. Because he wanted her to come here. Because he wanted to keep her safe.

She kept that idea centered in her mind as she stepped inside and locked the door behind her before dragging over a straight chair. Tipping it up, she wedged the top rung under the knob. If someone wanted to come in, she wasn't going to make it easy for them.

She could be locking Troy out, of course. But somehow she didn't think that was going to be the case.

HE STOOD in the shadows of the bedroom, one hand slipped into his pocket, the casual pose belying the electric tension coursing through him.

He'd chosen a spot with an excellent view of the sitting room, and his heart lurched when he saw the door to the hall open.

She had come! Because he'd asked her here, he hoped.

Still as a statue, he watched her lock the door behind her then drag over a chair and tip it under the doorknob.

Probably her eyes hadn't quite adjusted to the dark. But he had no such problem. Silently, he followed her progress as she crossed the rug and stepped into the bedroom.

The moment she'd entered his territory, he'd sensed a kind of humming in the air, a physical vibration that he recognized as the charged energy he'd felt when she stepped into the grove of trees.

Did she sense it, too? Was that why she suddenly hesitated, lifting her head and looking around like an animal smelling danger on the wind?

He knew the exact moment when her questing gaze found him standing in the corner.

Always before he'd stood behind her or come to her in the dark. This time was different. She could see him, and he felt her regard like a jolt of electricity.

For a few charged moments there was only the humming in the air. Then he heard a small, throat-clearing noise from her. When she spoke, he knew she was trying to control her voice. Still, it came out high and quavery.

"Troy! Your face…there's nothing wrong with it."

"That's right."

"Then why—?" She stopped in midsentence and changed the question. "What are you doing standing there like a cat burglar—trying to take a couple of months off my life?"

He liked the defiance in her voice, defiance that masked the undercurrent of anxiety.

"I'm being cautious. The way you are." He gestured toward the lamp. "But you didn't bring one of my best pieces of crystal to attack me, did you?"

"No."

"Then why don't you put it down?"

She shifted her gaze to the makeshift weapon in her hand, then shrugged and set it on the floor against the wall.

"Thank you for coming up here. That was brave of you."

"Brave!" She snorted. "I'm not brave. I'm being prudent. Someone was in my room while I was taking a shower. Was it you?''

He hesitated for a moment, considering a lie. Yet he had vowed to be honest with her—as honest as he could be. He gave a small shrug. ''Yes. Too bad the shower curtain is only translucent,'' he added as a small reassurance.

He saw her cheeks redden, liking the effect. She was so vital. So alive. He'd been dead inside until she'd arrived at Ravencrest and worked her unconscious magic on him.

''Living alone hasn't done much for your manners. Don't you know it's not nice to sneak into a woman's bathroom?''

''I couldn't resist you,'' he said simply. ''You draw me to you.''

''And you wanted me to come up here—after you got a good look at me.''

He chose to focus on the first part. ''Yes. You felt me calling you?''

She didn't answer the question. ''You could have helped me out with the computer password,'' she said instead.

He thought about that, trying not to let his frustration overtake him. Sometimes he felt strong, powerful. But it didn't take much to knock that confidence out from under him. It was several seconds before he answered. ''I don't know the password.''

''You forgot it?''

''I don't remember,'' he growled.

She might have pushed him on that. She'd pushed him before, demanding answers that he couldn't or didn't want to give. But he didn't allow her a chance.

He knew how to keep her from digging too deeply. He knew her vulnerabilities. And his own.

Slowly he crossed the room, watching her, giving her a chance to back away from him because deep in his heart he knew that asking anything from her that she didn't want to freely give was the worst kind of betrayal.

But she stayed where she was, her hands at her sides, her chin turned upward.

She was pretending calm, as he had when she'd first come in. But he heard the catch in her breath, saw the emotion simmering in her eyes.

The mixture of fear and anticipation was as strong in him as it was in her. He wanted this so badly. But what if it all went wrong? He set the fear aside and reached for her.

The first instant of contact branded him. He folded her close, wrapping himself in her wonderful scent, the heat of her body warming the hard shell of ice that had walled off his soul.

She was his salvation. His lifeline. And so much more. When he brought his mouth down to hers, it was like a current of heat and energy flowing into him.

With a low moan of need, he claimed her lips, angling his head to take her mouth in a wild, demanding kiss.

He was staking his claim. But he was instantly lost in the taste of her, the feel of her mouth on his, the lithe weight of her body in his arms. She was like the wind blowing off the ocean—strong and sweet, with an energy that crackled through him.

He'd watched her in the shower. Oh, yes, he'd watched her. Taken in her unconscious sensuality. Been mesmerized by the beautiful feminine curves of her. Seen the creamy skin of her breasts and the pink buds of her nipples. Followed droplets of water as they slid down her body, over her rounded buttocks or into the thatch of blond hair at the juncture of her legs.

He'd known he shouldn't be invading her privacy. But it had been impossible for him to turn away. And the sight of her had been like a flow of hot lava coursing through him.

He'd known then that he must hold her. Kiss her. Give her what pleasure he could give.

He felt her heart pounding in her chest, heard her shaky breathing as he moved his mouth over her lips, then pushed aside her silky hair and transferred his attentions to the tempting patch of skin below her ear.

She moaned, and he knew that he had her under his spell.

Then, heartbeats later, he felt her pushing against him, pushing him away.

"Troy." She gasped.

"I'm here."

"Lord, yes. You're here. But don't do this! You know you can swamp my senses when what we really need to do is talk."

He sighed. He wasn't going to get what he wanted. Not yet.

"Talk about what?" he asked, hearing the thickness of his own voice. There were so many subjects she could pick. He waited, the tension coursing through him.

"Helen."

"I don't want to talk about my sister." Or anything else, he silently added.

"We have to! It all goes back to Helen. She asked me to come here and find out what was wrong. She told me that you invited the Sterlings to Ravencrest. That you were—" She stopped and dragged in a breath. "Okay. I don't know how else to say this. She told me that you weren't yourself after Grace's death. You weren't paying enough attention to…your life. And you let the Sterlings take advantage of you."

Her words were an accusation, stabbing at him like a thin-bladed knife. After Grace had died, he had been drifting through his life in a fog. "That was true for a while," he muttered, then considered the other part of what she'd said. "But I didn't invite them. It was Helen. She wrote me and said they had nowhere else to go."

Bree stared at him as though he wasn't making sense. "I don't understand. She was the one who begged me to come and check things out because she said you'd asked the Sterlings here. And she was afraid they'd taken control of the estate."

He felt the words pound him like stones as he fitted this new information with one of their previous conversations. He'd remembered their idyllic summer together. And he'd remembered she was Helen's friend from school. But the two facts hadn't connected in his mind, even when she'd claimed Helen had sent her here. The implications of what that meant had finally filtered into his muzzy brain. Now his voice turned sharp, as pieces of a puzzle came together in a new way. "Wait a minute. How could she ask you here? I tried to get your address from her and she said she'd lost contact with you years ago."

Chapter Twelve

"What?" Bree gasped, her fingers digging into Troy's shoulders.

He stared down at her. "Lord, I wanted to see you again, so much. After I was free. But I couldn't find anyone named Bonnie Brennan who turned out to be you. And Helen said she couldn't help me. That was one of the reasons I was so depressed."

"I changed my name," she said.

"I know that now. You're Bree. It fits you better now that you're grown up."

She stared up at him, totally thrown off balance. Helen had never said that Troy had wanted to get together with her.

Confusion swirled in her brain. Confusion about Helen. About Troy. About her reason for being here.

"So did she make up the story about the Sterlings to get us back together?" she asked. "She always could come up with such complicated schemes. Remember that summer she wrote complaint letters to companies, pretending she was you? She watched you get all that mail. Some of the companies threatened to sue you and some sent you cases of products to make up for the deficiencies that you'd claimed you'd found. Only it wasn't you. And when you discovered it was Helen who'd caused all the uproar, you were so mad.''

He gave a harsh laugh. "Yeah, I remember that summer. She was twelve and I was fifteen.''

"So couldn't this be one of her elaborate schemes?'' she asked, hoping against hope that he'd agree.

"If she wanted to get us back together, she certainly took a roundabout route. All she had to do was give me your address and phone number.''

"Yes. She and I never lost touch.'' Bree let the implications sink in. "So are you saying she made the whole thing up about the Sterlings?'' she asked slowly. "Why would she do that?''

She saw him consider the questions.

He ignored the motivation part. "She didn't make up the whole thing,'' he said after long moments. "I think they did something bad.''

"What?''

"I'm not sure.''

"Hit you over the head and gave you partial amnesia, like in that scene you showed me. Only now your memory is coming back.''

"Yes,'' he murmured, but it was obvious his thoughts had turned inward. "Maybe it wasn't them,'' he said slowly.

"Tell me everything you remember,'' she pleaded.

"Bree, I've told you what I remember. And we've already wasted so much time. I don't want to waste any more talking about the Sterlings. Not when I've longed for you to come back to me,'' he said thickly, smothering her attempt at a protest by covering her lips with his.

The kiss was hot and thorough, and it took her breath away. She was feeling light-headed as he slid his lips away from hers to the sensitive line of her jaw and then the tender place at the top of her neck.

The part of her mind that still functioned told her to pull away again. They weren't finished with the conversation. And the conversation was important. If she kept asking questions, maybe he would remember more.

But coherence was rapidly deserting her. He had said he didn't want to waste any more time, and she understood that so well. Time with him had become precious.

Later. They could talk later.

She made a small whimpering sound in her throat, her hands finding the hem of his shirt and slipping underneath. As her palms slid against his skin, she heard him gasp.

"Yes," she whispered.

The feelings were so elemental. The intimacy staggering.

She had been here such a short time, but the passion between them had been building from the first night in her bed.

He had teased her, tantalized her.

"I want you naked," he whispered. "The way you were in the shower."

"Oh, yes."

His hands went to the front of her shirt. At first he fumbled as he slid the buttons open, but his touch became more sure as he continued the task. Then he was slipping the garment off her shoulders.

She helped him then, reaching around to snap the catch on her bra, lifting it away and sending it to join the shirt.

He bent to kiss her shoulders, the tops of her breasts; she arched against him, silently begging for more.

His hands were busy again, pulling off her slacks and panties, skimming them down her legs. She stepped out of the unwanted clothing and kicked it away, so that she stood naked in his arms—aroused but just a little uncertain.

She was totally exposed. He was still fully dressed. She wanted him naked, too, but when she tried to speak, her voice caught in her throat as his hands stroked her flanks, cupped her bottom, pulling her against his taut length, his body swaying with hers in an erotic rhythm that swamped her senses.

"You are so lovely," he whispered. "And so generous. You were always so generous. That was one of the things that attracted me to you. And that was how I lost you. Your mother got sick and you put her welfare before anything you wanted."

She couldn't speak. She could only nod, because that was the truth. Walking away from him back then had been the hardest thing she'd ever done. Yet she'd put duty before her own happiness.

"Let me love you. Let me love you now."

"Yes!" she cried. She had wanted him for so long, and now he was giving himself to her.

He scooped her up in his arms and carried her to the bed. With one hand, he pulled aside the covers, laying her on the crisp white sheet. Then he followed her down.

Her hands plucked at his shirt. "Troy, please, take your clothes off."

He rolled away long enough to rid himself of the shirt. Then he gathered her to him again, pressing her against his body. She reached up, winnowing her fingers through his thick hair, pulling his mouth to hers in a kiss that was sweeter than any they had exchanged before. The underlying passion sent heat shimmering through her.

As she kissed him, she tried to show him the depths of her feelings. She had given up any hope of getting together with him when she'd learned about his marriage. But she had never forgotten him, never stopped wondering what might have been between them.

Deep down she knew that was the real reason she had come to Ravencrest so eagerly, so recklessly. She was stronger than she'd been when she first knew him, more sure of what she wanted—no matter the risks. That was why she'd come back to this room that she'd been forbidden to enter. Helen had given her a chance to find Troy again, and she had seized the opportunity—and damn the consequences.

She was incapable of considering any consequences now. She had been unsure of him, afraid of him, even. But none of that mattered at this moment. She could only kiss him and stroke his strong back and shoulders, and lose herself in the building ecstasy of making love with him.

Finally. Finally it was their time.

When he dipped his head and took one of her pebble-hard nipples into his mouth, she moaned her pleasure and clasped him to her.

He brought her up, up to heights she had hardly imagined. His fingers stroked down her body, playing with the thatch of blond hair below her abdomen before slipping lower and parting her hot, slick feminine flesh.

"Oh, Troy," she rasped, clinging to him, almost overcome by the pleasure he was giving her.

Yet she needed to know he was sharing that pleasure as fully as she.

She reached for him, starting to slide her hand down the front of his body to the fly of his jeans. But he caught her fingers, stopped her downward progress.

"Troy, I want you with me," she breathed.

"I am with you. I'm right here. All the way." As he

spoke he grasped her small hands in one of his large ones, pulling them up and over her head, trapping her so that he could work his will.

"Hold on to the headboard," he murmured.

She did as he asked, her hands clenching and un-clenching on the brass bars.

He kissed her then as he began to stroke her once more, drinking in her little cries.

She was swept along on the tide of sensuality he had created. Unconsciously her hips rocked against his clever fingers as she sought maximum contact, maximum sensation.

Her reward was a surge of ecstasy that could only be sustained for a measured space of time—physical pleasure that built and built to an incredible peak of tension.

"Let go, sweetheart. Show me how good it feels." Two of his fingers slipped inside her, triggering a burst of erotic intensity that sent her spinning out of control into a wild, shattering climax.

She called out his name, her hands clenching tightly on the bars of the headboard, even as small aftershocks rippled through her inner muscles.

"Troy, please, I want to give you that pleasure, too." She lowered her arms and reached for him.

He bent, stopping her words with a long, deep kiss that seemed to say he was ready to allow her to return the joy he had given her. Then, just as she relaxed into the kiss, he pulled away from her.

She cried out at the sudden loss, even as she reached for him again, trying to bring him back. But she knew in the next moment that she was alone on the bed, alone in the room.

Totally alone.

She lay there breathing hard, trying to come back to

herself, knowing there was no use calling out to the man who had just given her so much physical pleasure—and then left her. The way he always left her. Now that she thought back over what had happened between them, she could see he had planned what he wanted to do. Carry her away in ecstasy, then disappear.

Moments ago she'd been flying as high as the stars. Now she fought the tears gathering in the backs of her eyes.

Damn him!

He had made her believe that he wanted her to come back to him. Was that a lie? Was he playing with her? Or worse, was he using her for his own purposes?

She squeezed her eyes shut, trying to make that idea go away. She desperately wanted to ask him what was going on. Why he had chosen that way to make love to her, and why he had left so suddenly. But she didn't even know if she could believe his answer.

She thought about going back to her own bed but she knew she would never sleep in that room, not now.

So she pulled up the covers and burrowed down into the warmth created by her own body. She actually slept for a few hours, then rose, determined to take some positive action.

It was still dark when she returned to her room, changed her clothing and left again, heading for the part of the house where Dinah's room and the schoolroom were located, in search of new sleeping quarters.

"So, Troy," she murmured in a low voice as she walked quietly down the hall, "what do you think about my changing bedrooms? If you don't approve, all you have to do is say so."

She didn't expect an answer, and she didn't get one,

even though she couldn't shake the feeling that he knew perfectly well what she was doing.

One door down from the sunporch, she found a small but charmingly decorated bedroom. It had only a small closet, which she considered a definite plus, and she checked it carefully to make sure there was no secret entrance. Then, before the rest of the household was awake, she packed up her clothing and toilet articles and moved them to the new location.

She was just putting her underwear in the dresser in the new room when the door burst open.

She almost jumped out of her skin, until she found herself facing a distressed-looking Mrs. Martindale.

The housekeeper's eyes widened when she saw Bree. "Why, it's you again! What are you doing in here?"

"I'm changing rooms."

"Why on earth? Wasn't the old one satisfactory?"

"It was fine. But it was too far away from Dinah. I want to be close to her. So I took the liberty of moving my things. I hope that's not an inconvenience."

"Oh, no. That's fine. I just couldn't imagine who was in here."

"Were you expecting a ghost?" Bree couldn't stop herself from asking.

The housekeeper laughed. "Of course not. You just gave me a start, but I guess it cuts both ways. You looked like you thought an ax murderer had come in."

Bree joined in the laughter. "Yes, well, this house can be kind of spooky."

Mrs. Martindale nodded, then said, "The bed in this room isn't made up. I can do that for you after breakfast."

"I don't want to put you to any extra trouble. I'll do it. Just show me where to find the linens."

"I'll bring them now." She left and returned a few minutes later with towels, sheets and pillowcases.

Bree kept herself busy making the bed and arranging the towels in the bathroom. Something kept nagging at her. Some fact she should match with some other fact. But whatever it was wouldn't come to her.

It was only a little past dawn when she finished making the bed, but she was too restless to sit still.

After pulling on a jacket, she went down the back stairs and out the door. She had told herself she just needed a breath of fresh air, but as soon as she stepped outside, she knew where she was going. Quickly she crossed the garden area, then stepped out onto the headlands. This early in the morning, mist rolled in off the ocean, making it difficult to see the edge of the cliff.

She knew that made for dangerous walking, but if she kept her gaze a few feet ahead of her, she could see the path she'd taken the day before.

Her hands were cold and she thrust them into her pockets, hearing the roar of the waves breaking against the cliffs as she walked away from the house.

She saw the grove of trees ahead and veered toward the left, plowing through the low-growing vegetation. Even in full daylight, the shadows under the canopy of branches had been spooky. With mist wafting around the moss-covered trunks, it was even spookier. For a moment she hesitated then she stepped out of the open area and under the trees, her breath coming hard and fast, as though she'd just run a race.

She stood quietly, waiting for her breathing to settle. When she decided she could hear something besides the air rushing in and out of her lungs, she listened.

She thought she picked up the deep, throbbing sound that she'd heard the first time she'd come running in here.

But now it seemed far away and she couldn't be sure she wasn't making it up.

With her heart pounding, she waited for the whirlwind of pine needles. But the air was still and heavy.

"Troy, I know you're there," she said. "I can feel you watching me."

Only the chirping of an unseen bird answered her.

"What are you, a coward?" she asked. "You take me to your bed and make love to me—if you want to call that making love—and then you can't deal with the rest of a relationship?"

She had deliberately challenged him, but he chose to ignore the goading words.

"So all you want is for me to get out of here and take Dinah," she said. "What am I supposed to do, steal Graves's keys?"

There was a small flicker in the air, a small whirlwind of pine needles and dust rising from the ground about twenty-five feet from her. She held her breath, waiting for more. Waiting to see Troy's image, the way she had before.

"And where would you suggest I look?"

An image came to her then, an image of a small building hidden in the shrubbery on the far side of the driveway from the house. She'd seen it from one of the windows, but she hadn't known that it had anything to do with Graves. Well, actually, it might not. She might simply have dredged up an answer when she expected something from Troy.

But she couldn't dispel the notion that it was he who had put the image in her mind.

"Thanks," she said, her gaze trained on the swirl of forest matter, her hand reaching out as though she could grab the eddying dust.

The wind puffed once more, sending pine needles into a spiral that flew several feet into the air then settled quickly as though it had never been there.

She tried to ignore her disappointment. The grove was dark and still.

"All right. I'll play it your way," she said. For now, she silently added. Turning, she started back toward the house, angling so that she would reach the spot where she imagined the shed was standing.

She slowed her steps as she came near the building, seeing a light shining through the window. Feeling like a sneak thief, she was creeping closer to have a look in one of the windows when the door opened and the man himself came out.

She waited for several minutes, torn between going inside and fearing that the handyman would reappear. But Graves didn't come back, and she decided that perhaps he had gone to breakfast. Still she hesitated, thinking it would be unfortunate to get caught here. But her urgency was too great. "Watch my back," she said to Troy as she stepped up to the door.

It was unlocked. She hurried inside, then took a furtive look around. The room was neat; she'd say that much for the man. Hand tools were arranged on a Peg-Board wall or in drawers. Power tools were on shelves, two heavy-duty power cords were neatly coiled on hooks and the broad wooden worktable was uncluttered. Sitting in the middle of it was a purple boom box that looked entirely out of place.

Drawn to it, she pressed the eject button and looked at the tape. "Rod Stewart's Greatest Hits."

If Graves was working with Helen, he could have played it to be spooky. She shook her head, surprised at how far her thinking had changed. Of course, there was another equally plausible explanation. Graves had been scared by the music, then brought the tape down here to see what was on it.

She pushed the cassette door closed again, turned down the volume and pressed the play button. The music was what she'd heard, all right.

She listened to only a snatch, then turned it off, remembering that she had come here looking for car keys. They weren't any place obvious, she decided as she inspected the various hooks on the Peg-Board wall, then began opening drawers.

But Troy had as good as told her they were here. Unless she was making up the whole silent communication.

She was just closing a drawer when she heard footsteps hurrying along the path outside.

Oh, God, Graves was coming back.

Chapter Thirteen

Bree had asked Troy to watch her back. Now she thought how useless that request had been. She was on her own and she had only seconds to decide what to do. Wildly she looked around, seeing that there was nowhere to hide in the small room except in the closet.

She'd been caught snooping around too many times already. And the idea of standing here to confront whoever was outside gave her a sick feeling. Quickly she pulled the closet door open and found that it didn't lead to a closet at all but to another entrance on the opposite side of the building.

She had just made her escape when the door she'd first entered eased open.

She didn't know who had come in until she moved to one of the windows and peered cautiously over the sill. It wasn't Graves. It was Abner Sterling, and he looked wild-eyed and frightened. Maybe Troy *had* tried to stop him from coming in, she thought as she watched Abner struggle to catch his breath.

After a few moments he began a routine very similar to her own—opening drawers and poking around on shelves.

With only a part of her face showing at the grimy

glass, Bree stayed where she was, ready to duck if the man looked as though he was going to turn in her direction.

He was searching for something and she was pretty sure he hadn't found it. He straightened, standing with his hands on his hips in the middle of the room. His gaze flicked to the boom box and he strode toward it, pressing down on the play button without bothering to check the tape.

When Rod Stewart blared out, he stared at the machine with narrowed eyes. So had he heard Rod Stewart up in Troy's room, too?

As she watched, he ejected the cassette, which he slipped into his pocket. Apparently he didn't care whether or not Graves knew the cassette was missing.

He spent several more minutes searching the workshop, being careful to put everything back where he'd found it.

She had a bad moment when he looked toward the door where she'd exited, perhaps considering going out that way. But he turned and went back out the other door.

Bree waited where she was, wondering what she was going to do. She hadn't found any keys. But she wasn't going back in there now. She'd made a lucky escape once and she didn't want to risk meeting anyone else here.

She sighed, thinking it was a long walk into town— too long for Dinah.

Back at the house, she entered the dining room to find Nola looking impatiently toward the door.

Dinah was at the table, hunched over her cereal bowl.

"Where were you?" Nola snapped.

"I went for a walk before breakfast."

"We didn't know where you were," Nola stated,

clearly annoyed. "Mrs. Martindale says you changed bedrooms."

"Yes, I wanted to be closer to Dinah," she said, smiling at the little girl who was watching the exchange from under lowered lashes. Then she turned her attention back to Nola. "Did you need me for something?"

"As a matter of fact, yes. Mr. Hirsch from the school board called. He wants to make sure that Dinah's studies are conforming to the county curriculum. Are they?"

"As far as I can ascertain," Bree answered.

"Well, he'll be out here at two this afternoon to inspect the schoolroom, look at your lesson plans and interview you."

"Isn't that rather short notice?"

"That's the point. You're supposed to be prepared."

"Right," Bree agreed, wondering if she really was in compliance. She hadn't been here very long and all she had to go on was the material that the previous teacher had left.

Lord, something else to worry about!

"I'd better make sure everything's ready," she said, then turned to Dinah. "When you finish your breakfast, come up to the classroom."

"Aren't you going to eat?" the child asked.

"I'll just grab something and take it up."

She fixed herself a cup of coffee and a piece of toast, then hurried upstairs.

She should have looked at the local curriculum requirements, she thought as she began searching through the supply closet shelves, trying to locate thick, notebook-size manuals.

"Why didn't you warn me about this?" she muttered, speaking to Troy as she scrambled through stacks of materials. "You could at least show me where the stuff is."

The room remained silent and she stood for a moment, listening with her ears and her other senses. Since Troy had abandoned her in his bed last night, she couldn't shake the notion that he was keeping tabs on her. And apparently she couldn't stop addressing him as if he were in the room.

"Don't you want to get involved?" she challenged.

She got an immediate answer, but not from the unseen man she was addressing.

"Who are you talking to?" a small voice asked. It was Dinah who had chosen that moment to walk into the room.

Bree felt her cheeks heat. After waiting a beat she turned. "Probably it sounds silly, but I've gotten into the habit of talking to your dad. Even when I'm not sure he's really around."

"It doesn't sound silly. Sometimes I do it," the girl said. "It makes me feel better. But I only started after he came in the night and talked to me."

"Just now I was asking him where to find the curriculum, but he didn't answer me. Do you happen to know where it is?" Bree asked.

"On the bottom shelf. Right over there," the child pointed. "I remember when Miss Carpenter put it away."

As Bree took a quick look at the material, she felt a surge of relief. Then she looked back at Dinah.

"Thank you. This is just what I need. Now I'd better go over this stuff before I have to see Mr. Hirsch."

After setting Dinah up with some exercises from her reading workbook, she paged through the curriculum, comparing it to the work that had been assigned and to upcoming lessons. To her relief, it looked as if they were in compliance.

She gathered up some of Dinah's previous exercises

and had just put them in a folder with upcoming lesson plans when Mrs. Martindale appeared in the doorway, looking flustered.

"He's here early."

Bree took in the housekeeper's anxious visage. Obviously she was worried about passing inspection.

"Is he pretty strict about following the rules?" she asked.

Mrs. Martindale lowered her voice. "He had some complaints when I was supervising Dinah's education."

"It's not exactly your field," Bree assured her.

"But he wants to make sure everything's back on the right track."

"Well, let's go down and reassure him," Bree answered with all the confidence she could muster, considering that she wasn't sure how the interview was going to come off. For a moment she hesitated, then she turned to Dinah. "Do you want to come with us?"

The child considered the question. "I guess I'd like to stay up here."

"That's fine." Bree looked at the sheets of paper on the desk. "Probably you should keep working on your lessons, in case he wants to see what you're doing during school hours today."

Dinah nodded, then bent to her work again.

Bree followed Mrs. Martindale to the sitting room, thinking that she might have been handed an opportunity to get out a message.

But when she reached the meeting place, her hopes dimmed. She found Nola waiting with a small, gray-haired man who was sipping from a cup of tea. On the plate in front of him was a selection of cookies that the housekeeper had apparently assembled in his honor.

He looked up, and she saw a round face and piercing blue eyes that stopped her in her tracks.

"Mr. Hirsch, this is Miss Brennan, the new teacher who's been engaged for Dinah."

Having decided that she should seem confident, even if her insides were quivering, Bree crossed the room and shook his hand. "I've brought you some of Dinah's recent work," she said, "and lesson plans for the next few months."

After handing over the folder, she took a chair across the coffee table from Hirsch and sat with her hands folded in her lap, a strategy that kept her audience from seeing them tremble. She noticed that Nola didn't offer her tea, although there was an extra cup on the tray.

Hirsch picked up a cookie, chomping appreciatively as he began to page through the materials she'd given him.

Bree held her breath, waiting for his verdict and wondering what she was going to do if he didn't approve of the current situation.

"Very good," he finally said. "Yes, this is what I was looking for."

The pronouncement seemed to do wonders for Nola's tension level. Even Mrs. Martindale, who had been hovering in the doorway, departed.

"Of course, I'll have to review this material in my office before I write you an official letter," he said. "But I think I won't need to make another home visit for several months."

"That's good," Nola answered.

Feeling as if she'd gotten an outstanding grade on her college board exams, Bree let out a small sigh. "Do you want to see the schoolroom?" she asked, thinking that might be a way to get him alone.

He shook his head. "I've seen it. I assume there haven't been any major changes."

"No," Nola answered.

Mr. Hirsch sipped his tea and ate several more cookies before standing. "It was nice meeting you," he said to Bree.

"Yes. Thank you for stopping by. I should get back to Dinah," she added, leaving the room, still hoping she could get a few moments alone with the man. She didn't know him, but he seemed to be conscientious about his job, and perhaps he could help her and Dinah get away.

Instead of heading upstairs, she went to the back door and slipped outside. It was still cool and she shivered in her thin shirt as she walked quickly around the house toward the front driveway, where she saw a small black car parked.

Hirsch came out and she started to hurry toward him. Then movement at the side of the driveway caught her eye and she spotted Graves pruning bushes.

An unladylike curse sprang to her lips. Every damn bush on the estate looked as though it hadn't been pruned in years, and now here was Graves working away as if he performed this service on a regular basis.

Probably he'd been sent out here to make sure she didn't get to Hirsch, she decided, thinking how paranoid that sounded. Yet she couldn't come up with any other explanation.

She thought about marching to the driveway anyway and asking for a private word with the school official. But that would certainly tip her hand—perhaps without doing any good. All she knew about Hirsch was from one brief meeting. He'd gotten a favorable impression of her from the work she'd presented. But that could change if she came across as an hysterical female and he went back to Nola with his assessment.

Her lower lip clamped between her teeth, she watched him get into his car and disappear down the driveway.

Her pace was slow as she returned to the schoolroom. Under her breath she began talking to Troy.

"Well, the school board isn't going to toss me out on my ear," she told him. "But I'm no closer to getting out of here than I was when they locked the gate behind me. Any suggestions?"

He didn't answer, and she cut off the one-sided conversation as she stepped into the room.

Looking around, she was seized by a moment of panic when she didn't immediately see Dinah at the desk. Then she spotted the girl sitting in the love seat in the small alcove at one side of the room. A large book was spread across her lap.

As the child glanced up and saw her, a pinched look captured her face.

Bree walked quickly toward her.

"I—I know I'm supposed to be working," the small voice quavered. "But I was afraid you'd have to leave."

"No. Everything's fine," Bree said, thinking that at least the statement applied to her tenure here.

"I'm glad," Dinah whispered.

"Me, too."

Slipping onto the love seat beside the little girl, she looked down at the book. It was a picture album.

She saw several photos of Dinah with Troy. Then Dinah with Grace.

"That's your mom?" Bree asked as she studied the photographs, thinking that Grace London had been very attractive.

"Yes," the girl whispered. "I look at pictures of her

because when I don't, I start to forget what she looked like.''

Bree's heart squeezed. Quietly she slipped her arm around the child and felt gratified as Dinah leaned into her.

"Can I look through your album?" she asked.

"Yes."

Though they were sitting on a sofa pushed against the wall, Bree had the feeling that someone was behind her, watching as she turned the pages.

"You were a very cute baby," Bree said, hearing the tightness in her own voice. "And you've turned into a very pretty little girl."

"That's what Daddy said."

Bree nodded then quietly asked, "How did your mom and dad get along?"

Dinah was silent for several moments and Bree was afraid she wasn't going to answer.

Finally she said, "Sometimes I would hear them fighting, and it would make me sad—and afraid."

"Yes. That would be upsetting and scary."

The child nodded.

Bree took in a breath and let it out while considering her next words. "I know your daddy was upset about your mom getting killed in that automobile accident. Do you know what happened? I mean, do you know who was driving the car?"

She kept her breath even, wondering what the child was going to say.

BREE WASN'T THE ONLY ONE who wanted to hear how Dinah would answer. From his hiding place Troy focused on the little girl, waiting anxiously. He knew Dinah had heard the adults talking. What did she know?

He had been drawn here by the child. By the woman. Yet he realized that he wasn't going to do either one of them any good. He would only pull them down to his level, and he couldn't let that happen.

Last night he had fulfilled one of his most enduring fantasies—holding Bree in his arms. He had wanted to give her pleasure. He had told himself that making love with her had been a good thing. Now he wasn't so sure. She wanted to help him. But she couldn't help. There was only one thing she could do for him—get the child away from Ravencrest.

But Bree had spent the early morning looking for him. She was talking to him as she walked around the house, for Lord's sake. And searching for him wasn't where she should be putting her energy.

Conflicting needs warred within him and he thought about showing himself to Bree and Dinah now. He could step out of hiding, communicate directly. But that would only give them hope that things were going to change. And as pieces of his memory had fitted themselves back into place, he had finally realized that nothing could change. Not for him. And not for them.

He had made some bad mistakes in the past. He wasn't going to compound those mistakes now. Not with Dinah. And not with Bree. Which meant treading carefully—and making sure that neither one of them thought they were going to live happily ever after with him.

So he waited—listening, watching and trying to figure out how he could make things come out right for the two people he had come to care about most in the world.

"I WASN'T SUPPOSED TO BE listening," Dinah said tentatively.

"It's okay. I know kids listen in on adult conversations. I used to do it when I was little, too."

Dinah nodded, but she lowered her voice as she said, "I heard my daddy talking to Mr. Alexander about it. He didn't know I was spying on them."

"Who is Mr. Alexander?"

"Our minister."

"Oh. What did your daddy say to him?"

"It was private."

She stroked her hand over the child's slender shoulder. "But it would help me to understand if you can tell me what your daddy said."

"Why?"

"Because I'm trying to figure out what's happening at Ravencrest."

Dinah nodded. "He said Mommy was driving, but they were fighting, so he felt like it was his fault."

Bree stroked the child's shoulder. "Thank you for telling me."

"Did that help you understand?"

"Yes," she answered. At least it confirmed what Troy had told her, although it didn't explain a lot of other things, of course. But Troy had been upset and had turned to his minister for comfort. Under the circumstances, it seemed unlikely that Troy would lie to the man.

For several moments she focused on the book, turning the pages, studying pictures of the family. When you looked casually at the photographs, the people looked happy. But if you examined the images more carefully, you picked up signs of tension.

She saw a tightness in Troy's jaw and a sullen look she came to recognize in Grace's eyes. They seemed like people who weren't entirely comfortable with each other but were making the best of a bad situation. And the strain was getting to be too much for them.

The photos stopped abruptly, leaving a dozen blank pages at the back of the book.

"I wish there were more pictures," Dinah said.

"Yes." She wanted to say something else comforting, but she wasn't sure what.

They were both quiet for a moment, then Bree reached into her pocket and pulled out the key that she'd discovered taped to the bottom of the desk drawer. She'd kept it with her since she'd found it. "There's something else you might be able to help me with," she said, holding it up. "Do you know what this key unlocks?"

The child stared at it. "I've seen Daddy with that key," she finally said. "I think it opens his strongbox."

Bree felt her heart thump in her chest. "Where does he keep his strongbox?"

"In his room."

Where she'd been the night before. Where he'd made love to her—at least as far as he was willing to go before he left her alone in bed. She'd silently vowed not to go there again. But now things had changed. She wasn't going there to meet him. She was going to look for the strongbox.

Chapter Fourteen

Once again Bree found herself sitting on her bed, waiting for the house to settle down so she could do what had been forbidden. Go to Troy's room.

It was a risk she didn't want to take, because the better she got to know Dinah, the more she liked the child. If she got kicked out of Ravencrest, she felt like she'd be throwing the little girl to the wolves.

But at the same time the key was burning a hole in her pocket. She'd been sent here to find out what was wrong, and whatever was in the strongbox might provide the answer. Ultimately that might be the only way to help Dinah.

"Damn you, Troy," Bree murmured as she slipped out of her room and headed down the hall. "You've put me in a pretty uncomfortable situation."

There was a stirring in the air, similar to the vibrations she'd felt in the grove but more subtle. The atmosphere around her seemed to thicken and she felt as though her steps were slowed by some invisible force.

"Stop it," she muttered. "I'm going to your room, whether you like it or not."

"What about Dinah?" Troy's voice whispered from

some hidden vantage point, his question echoing her own uncertainty.

"What about her?"

"You can't risk getting fired."

"That's right. So do something about it!" she challenged.

There was a breathless moment when nothing apparently happened. Then the air in the hallway changed, so that she no longer felt trapped in molasses. Now the sensation was entirely different, as though she were in the middle of an invisible bubble that moved with her as she made her way down the hall and then up the stairs.

It might be an illusion, but she felt that inside the space nobody could see her, although she didn't want to put the theory to the test. So she hurried along, staying in the shadows as best she could.

When she came to the back stairway, she heard voices and stopped abruptly.

It was Abner and Nola talking again. Last night they'd seemed on edge. Tonight the effect was magnified.

The protective bubble seemed to pull closer around her, as if Troy had taken her in his arms. She felt as if she were leaning into his strength as she pressed back against the wall.

Nola was shouting at Abner. "I can't take it anymore. That crazy session with Hirsch was the last straw. I'm tired of playing this role. I'm getting out of here, with or without you!"

"And going where? Maybe if I'd found Graves's stash of money, we could have done something. But not now."

Bree blinked. Abner had been prowling around looking for cash?

"Too bad," Nola continued. "Because I have to get away from this horrible place. Away from the ghost and that damn imperious housekeeper. So you get us out of here, or I'm going alone.''

''Don't act like this is my fault!''

The tone of his voice made the hairs on the back of Bree's neck prickle. He was so angry at his wife, she shuddered to think what he'd do if he realized someone was standing in the hall listening to them.

It was almost as if Troy caught her thought and used the powers she'd observed outside. In the next moment she felt a gust of wind spring up in the stairwell.

She could see nothing but she felt a wave of cold air rush down the steps, toward the couple in the hall below.

On the first floor she heard Nola gasp. ''What was that?''

''Hell if I know. It's like when I was going to Graves's shed to look for the money.''

The voices had been close, now they moved quickly away. As Bree strained her ears, the sound of the conversation faded and she was left standing alone in the hallway.

Well, not alone.

She still felt Troy's presence.

''Thank you,'' she murmured, the words barely audible.

''I didn't do much,'' he answered in the same low tone. Or maybe she only imagined the small exchange. Maybe she was going batty and imagining a lot of things. Like a hurricane inside the house.

Lips clamped together, she hurried down the hall to his room. ''I assume you've unlocked the door for me this time,'' she whispered under her breath as she reached for the knob.

It turned easily in her hand.

Once she had been afraid to lock herself in here with

a madman. Now she turned without hesitation and flipped the latch.

For several heartbeats she stood facing the door, feeling the darkness of the chamber pressing against her back. Then, squaring her shoulders, she pivoted to face the room. This was the one place where she'd actually seen Troy. Well, here and in the grove. But in this room the lines of his body had not been obscured by the whirling leaves. He had been real. Solid. Warm. Loving. Until he'd slipped away like a thief in the night.

"You're here, aren't you? So let me see you," she said. "Or are you playing games with me? The way you played games with Miss Carpenter. Why don't you make it easy for me and show me where to find the strongbox?"

She waited with her heart pounding. For a moment she was sure he wasn't going to answer her. Then she heard a faint noise and turned toward the closet. In the next breath the door opened and he stepped into the darkened room.

Her heart leaped. "Troy!"

Now that he was here, he came to her swiftly, taking her into his arms, holding her tightly. And she clasped him just as tightly, leaning into his warmth and strength, breathing in his familiar scent.

"I didn't play games with Miss Carpenter," he growled. "Well, I did, but not what you think. She and Nola got into some pretty strange discussions about the ghost. Sexual discussions."

"Nola tried to do that with me."

"I know. I didn't want Dinah hearing that kind of talk. So I decided to scare Miss Carpenter away."

"Oh."

"I'd scare you away, too, if I could."

"Well, I can't just leave. I can't exactly walk back to town with Dinah."

He nodded against the top of her head.

"Do you know who disabled my car?"

"Graves. I saw him."

"Why didn't you stop him?"

"I didn't want to be seen."

The conversation was going in circles as it had so often with Troy. By this time she'd learned that if he didn't want to deal with a subject, they weren't going to get anywhere with it. She sighed. "Are you going to show me where to find the strongbox?"

"Later."

There was a decisiveness in the way he said it, a strength she'd only sensed at their earlier encounters.

Bending, he captured her mouth in a kiss that tasted of urgency and raw male power—power that swept her along in its sensual spell.

She had come here on important business—*his* business. She had been angry with him for leaving the bed last night before she had gotten what she wanted. Yet now that she was in his arms, once again he worked his sexual magic on her.

In the back of her mind she knew that the sensual assault was deliberate, that he wasn't going to give her time to think. Not now.

She had vowed not to fall under his spell again. But apparently his special powers extended into the erotic realm, because she couldn't even remember why she had come here, except to find him. All she wanted at this moment was the deep rich taste of him, the thrilling feel of his hands on her body.

When he lifted his head, they were both breathing in hard, uneven gasps.

"Last time," she stammered, "I wanted more from you."

"And I couldn't give it to you. Not then."

A deep, overwhelming disappointment seized her. But in the next moment he soothed it away.

"This time will be different."

"Why?"

"Because when you give to me, you give me your power."

She didn't exactly understand what he meant but she wanted to believe that he trusted her in a way he hadn't trusted her before.

When he took her hand and led her into the bedroom, she went willingly. Moonlight streamed through the window, giving her enough light to see him. Maybe because she was still a little afraid that he'd disappear into thin air, she grasped the front of his shirt and began opening buttons, then slipped her hand inside, flattening her palm against his warm flesh.

She loved the hard muscles she felt. Loved the springy hair under her touch. Loved the way he sucked in his breath when her fingers stroked over his nipples.

Quickly she unbuttoned the shirt the rest of the way, then pushed it off his shoulders and onto the floor. When she reached for the hem of her own knit top, he stopped her hand.

"Let me," he growled, his voice rough as he dragged the garment over her head. Working quickly and efficiently, he got rid of her bra in almost the same motion.

She felt exposed and vulnerable, standing there naked to the waist. She watched his hands move in slow motion as he reached toward her breasts, then forgot everything else as his palms cupped her.

"You are so beautiful. So feminine," he murmured as

he touched and stroked her, his fingers cresting over her nipples, wringing a cry of pleasure from her.

Then he folded his arms around her back, bringing her against him—not tightly, just so that he could sway her in his embrace, stroking her breasts against the hair of his chest. It was exquisite. Arousing. So good that she could hardly stand.

He steadied her with one hand as the other removed her slacks and panties.

She wanted him naked, too. She had never seen him naked, she realized. Always before he had kept his body hidden from her. So she reached out and unhooked the snap at the top of his jeans, then held her breath as she waited for him to object. Instead he bent to find her mouth with his, and while he kissed her, she lowered his zipper. Reaching inside, she pressed her palm against his erection, gratified by his swift, indrawn breath. Quickly then she got rid of his jeans and briefs and stepped back to look at him.

He was magnificent. Fully aroused and very male. But he cut short her visual tour as he folded her back into his arms, sighing deeply as the naked length of her body settled against his.

They swayed together in the center of the room, touching and kissing and making small exclamations as their hands and lips explored each other and gave pleasure.

She felt her blood singing, felt sweet pressure building inside her.

"Take me to bed," she said, hearing the thick, shaky timbre of her voice.

"Oh, yes," he agreed, his fingers moving in a sensual pattern across her back as his mouth played with hers, demonstrating his expertise with a kiss. As she clung to him for support, his lips traveled lower, teasing her neck, her collarbone, the tingling flesh where her neck met her shoulder.

When she swayed on her feet again, he eased them toward the bed, pulling aside the covers so they could slip between the sheets.

He looked slightly dazed, as if he couldn't believe they were really here together, naked in his bed.

But it was true. Caught by a giddy sense of wonder, she wrapped her arms around his neck.

"You're shaking."

"So are you."

Whatever else she might have said turned into a long sigh of pleasure as his hands came back to her breasts, lifting them, then drawing circles that grew smaller and smaller as they converged on her nipples.

He was teasing her, building her anticipation. She gave him a pleading cry before he finally captured the hardened centers between his thumbs and fingers, eliciting another exclamation from her that was close to a sob.

He followed the caress with his lips and she cupped his dark head, caressing his thick hair, murmuring his name as he pleasured her.

He rolled her to her back and she smiled up at him, reaching to stroke the hair away from his forehead. It was just a bit too long, and she thought that perhaps later she could trim it for him.

But it was difficult to hang on to a coherent thought when his fingers found the moist, throbbing center of her.

She wanted to close her eyes and cling to him, but a small edge of panic threatened to intrude.

Last time he had tricked her. This time she wasn't going to let it end in the same way.

Sliding her hand down his body, she found the hard shaft of his erection again, closing her fingers around him, stroking a sensual pattern that she knew would bring her what she wanted.

"Troy, this time I want you inside me when I come."

"Yes."

He moved over her, his legs opening hers, and she felt that wonderful hard shaft press against her, into her, his body staking its claim on hers.

She kept her eyes open, kept them on his face, watching the tight pleasure she saw there. The intensity of it took her breath away.

He smiled down at her, then lowered his head to kiss her softly, tenderly. Shifting slightly, he found her breast with his fingers, caressing her, adding to her pleasure.

When he moved his hips it was slowly, deliberately, maddeningly.

Her body clamored for release. But he kept the pace where he wanted it, using his body and his hands and his mouth to bring her to an aching pinnacle of need.

"Troy... Oh, Troy, please," she cried.

He took mercy on her then, quickening the rhythm, wringing a deep, glad cry from her as an explosion of pleasure tore through her.

He gasped her name as his body convulsed above hers, and she clung tightly to his shoulders, thinking now that he had claimed her for his own.

Aftershocks of pleasure rippled through her as he held her in his arms. When he moved to her side, she snuggled against him, drifting as her hands tenderly stroked his slick skin.

"Thank you," she murmured, then took a chance and added, "I've waited years for that."

"So have I."

"Don't leave me. I don't want to wake up and find you've vanished."

His embrace tightened around her. "Sleep," he murmured.

She nestled down beside him, feeling more fulfilled and peaceful than she had in years.

None of the questions and problems had gone away, but because she wanted this time with Troy, she only burrowed against him, then lost herself in sleep.

Her slumber was deep and untroubled, perhaps because Troy held her in his arms. Just as the first light of dawn crept into the room, the gentle touch of his fingers on her cheek woke her.

Her eyes blinked open.

"It's time to go," he whispered.

"You're right. I shouldn't push my luck by staying any longer." She sat up and as she smoothed her hair back from her forehead, she remembered why she'd come here in the first place. "I forgot about looking for the strongbox."

"We had better things to do last night. The strongbox is behind a panel on the right side of the closet," he said, as if the hiding place were of little importance. "About three feet from the door."

She stared at him. "How do I get into it?"

"You just press on the wall there, and it will open."

When she started to scramble out of bed, he caught her wrist in his big hand. "It's not going anywhere."

"Are you going to tell me what's inside?" she demanded.

"My birth certificate, my marriage license." He stopped.

"Hardly worth hiding."

"Some stuff of Helen's."

"Helen! What does that have to do with you?"

"You can figure that out later. But right now you need to come outside with me."

She stared at him uncertainly. He'd made wonderful love to her a few hours ago, and she thought—no, she hoped—that everything had changed. But he was still acting the way he had since she'd first arrived: evasive, secretive.

She sighed. "I don't suppose you want to tell me what's so important outside?"

At least he looked regretful. "It's not the easiest thing to explain. You'd better come with me."

She didn't like the tone of his voice and she wanted to protest, yet she felt his sense of urgency.

She wanted to tell him what she had said before: if he was in some kind of trouble, she could help. But she didn't even know if that was true. Maybe there was nothing she could do. So she slowly got out of bed and began searching for the clothing they'd scattered around the floor.

She found his shirt first and silently handed it to him, her fingers lingering on his for just a moment.

Then she snatched up her own slacks and underwear.

He was dressed first, waiting while she went into the bathroom.

Back in the bedroom, he led her to the closet, then past the clothing hanging on the rod at the back. She wasn't really surprised to find a secret passage there, considering he'd appeared and disappeared through the closet several times. There was a flashlight hanging by a loop at the side of the doorway. He picked it up, playing it along the floor as they followed the tunnel downward.

First they came to what looked like a blank wall. Troy worked some hidden mechanism there, too, ushering her into another passageway that revealed itself.

A bunch of underground tunnels should look the same, but she suspected she'd been in this one before.

"Does this lead to the closet in my old bedroom?" she asked.

"Yes."

"So that's how you've been getting into my room so easily!"

He didn't comment, only led her along the stone passageway to the place where the tunnel made an abrupt turn. She realized she'd always kept to the right-hand wall. The left would have been a better choice, she noted as he opened a panel then ushered her into still another passageway.

"Who needed all these tunnels?" she asked.

"Smugglers. My grandfather had a nice illegal import business."

She wanted to ask more questions, but she was using all her energy to keep up with him. Ahead of her she could hear waves pounding against the shore, and when they came to stone steps, the surface was damp.

He took her arm, holding her tightly as they climbed to an opening just under the level of the cliff.

Below was a sheer drop to roiling water crashing against jagged rocks. One false step and you'd be dashed to death by the waves pounding the rugged shoreline.

She shrank back.

"It's okay. I won't let you fall," he said, and she remembered that other time when he'd caught her in mid-air.

She reached for his hand, her trust in him absolute as he led her up a rocky path to an indentation in the cliff wall that was much too high for her to scale on her own.

"Let me go first. Then I'll help you."

Detaching his hand from hers, he pulled himself up. Then he reached down for her.

She grabbed on to his solid flesh, knowing he was doing most of the work. Still, it was difficult to make those last few yards.

When they reached the top of the cliff, she stood in the shadow of a large huckleberry bush, breathing hard and looking back the way they'd come, thinking she never would have made it by herself.

Troy kept his arm around her, staring out at the churning water. "I always loved this place," he said. "I love the sound of the waves and the power of nature."

"Yes, it's beautiful."

"If Grace could have moved the house a couple of miles inland, she would have done it."

"You're kidding."

He shook his head, his expression regretful. "Come on. We'd better—"

He stopped abruptly, then thrust her roughly down behind a huckleberry bush, hunkering beside her, his hand clamping over her mouth as she tried to ask what he was doing.

Moments later she heard footsteps coming along the path. Apparently someone else was out and about early this morning.

She heard a voice and as the person came closer, she realized it was Graves.

Apparently he was talking to himself, muttering something she couldn't distinguish. Still, the tone of his voice made goose bumps rise on her arms.

She edged closer to Troy, comforted by the solid feeling of his body, the warmth of his skin.

Graves passed by the huckleberry bush where they were hiding.

For long moments neither Bree nor Troy moved. Finally she risked a peek around the foliage and saw the man's retreating figure. Still, if he turned around, he would see them. She didn't want to confront him and she was pretty sure Troy didn't want to give his presence away, so she waited until the handyman had passed into the garden and disappeared from view.

When Graves had exited the scene, Troy got to his feet and started through the scrubby, windblown vegetation that covered the headlands.

"Wait!"

She might as well have been talking to the sea. Running to catch up, she saw that they were only fifty yards from the grove of trees.

So the exit from the tunnels was near Troy's grove, which made it easy for him to get there—then back to the house when he was finished putting on a show out here for the Sterlings. Well, not just the Sterlings. Probably Mrs. Martindale and Graves, too.

She might have remarked on that, but his lips were set in a grim line. Apparently he wasn't happy about this little expedition, yet he was taking her here anyway.

They climbed over a fallen log, then plunged into the twilight under the trees. He led her across a patch of ground to a little clearing.

"There," he said, pointing to a spot where she could see a slight indentation in the earth. "That's why they don't come here."

The way he said it made her skin go icy.

"What is it?"

"Troy London's grave."

Chapter Fifteen

Bree felt as though a wrecking ball had hit her square in the chest, knocking all the air out of her lungs. She gasped, grappling with the enormity of what he had just said.

Troy London's grave!

It was too much to believe. Too much to absorb. And her only defense was a quick, decisive denial.

She swung toward Troy and grasped him by the shoulders. "Stop it! What are you trying to do? Did you know Graves was going to come walking along the cliff? Did the two of you cook this up?"

He stared down at her, his gaze intense and regretful. "No."

"Troy, I'm tired of this. Tired of your playing games. Tired of your saying something one minute and something else the next. If you can't be straight with me, then leave me alone."

"All right."

She hadn't meant it in literal terms. It had simply been her anger and her frustration—and her fear—talking. But Troy chose to take her at her word. He wrenched away from her, stumbled once, then dashed through the underbrush.

Wide-eyed, she started after him, shouting for him to stop. "Wait. I didn't mean it. Come back."

He didn't answer. Instead a gale-force wind rose up to hold her back, sending pine needles and other materials from the floor of the grove whirling in her face. Dust hit her eyes and she cried out, putting up her arm for protection, even as she tried to struggle forward. The whirlwind came fast and furious, tearing at her clothing, obscuring all vision, so that clouds of debris spun around her, rising to a frantic crescendo that roared in her ears like the howl of a lost soul in agony. Moments later, it was all over and she was alone in the grove.

"Troy!" she screamed, screamed until her throat was raw. But she already knew it would do her no good. He was gone again.

Only this time it was after they'd made love, when she'd thought that everything had changed. Well, not everything. At least she'd assumed that he was ready to work with her, not against her.

Now he had taken the first opportunity to let her know that she'd simply been operating on wishful thinking.

The new dishonesty made her angry. And, as she had when he'd shown her the grave, she focused on the anger, because there was no alternative. If she let go of the anger, she would be left with raw, blinding terror.

The night before, in the bedroom, when Troy had been kissing and caressing her, she'd felt as though her legs wouldn't hold her weight.

She felt like that now. Sinking to a fallen log, she huddled there, feeling her heart beating wildly in her chest.

He'd shown her Troy London's grave but he'd been standing next to her when he'd said it. It couldn't be his grave. It had to be a hoax. But at least now she knew the kind of thing he had in mind. He had been hiding out for weeks, probably because he'd lost all his money in those bad stock investments. Or maybe it was worse than that. Maybe he'd done something highly illegal to try to get his fortune back and it had all blown up in his face. He wasn't planning to stay around much longer. He wanted people to think he was dead, so he could disappear permanently. She wasn't part of his plans. He had been saying goodbye last night.

The scenario didn't make perfect sense, but it was the best she could conjure up, since there was no way to wrap her mind around the alternative.

It was several minutes before she was able to push herself to her feet. Then, resolutely, she started back to the house, unsure what she was going to do when she got there.

As she neared the back door, another thought intruded. She'd been so overwhelmed that she'd forgotten all about the strongbox!

Slipping her hand into her pocket, she was relieved to find the key. Now on a mission, she was about to charge inside the house when she checked her reflection in one of the windowpanes beside the door. She couldn't see much in the makeshift mirror, but what she could see wasn't pretty. Leaning forward, she picked several pine needles out of her hair, then tried to finger-comb her curls.

The hasty grooming hadn't done much good. She looked as though she'd been in a hurricane.

Well, she'd been out on the headlands, she reminded herself, where the wind was always blowing. That was a good excuse for her disheveled looks.

Slipping inside, she made her way toward the back

stairs. She'd almost reached her goal when Mrs. Martindale stepped out of a doorway.

"My word, you do look a fright," she said.

"I was out for a walk, and the wind was blowing pretty badly."

The housekeeper gave her a studied look. "You're getting to be quite a morning walker."

Bree cocked her head. Was the housekeeper keeping track of her habits? Great!

"Well, I'm probably still on east coast time. I'm often up early, and it's good to get some fresh air."

"You didn't see Graves by any chance, did you?"

Bree caught the woman's tension. "No," she answered quickly.

"I went to his room. He wasn't there. I need him to empty the garbage. He should have done it last night and now the can's full. I'm afraid I'll hurt my back if I try to lift it."

"If I see him, I'll tell him you're looking for him."

"Thank you. And you don't want to be late for breakfast. I'm making my hot cross buns. They're best right out of the oven."

"That sounds wonderful," Bree answered, then hurried up the steps to the room where she'd moved her belongings. After a quick shower, she pulled on fresh slacks and a beige knit top, then slipped back into the hall, thinking that if she moved quickly, she could get a look at the strongbox before breakfast.

As she had the night before, she heard voices and went stock-still. Again she recognized Abner Sterling. But he wasn't talking to his wife.

"What have you done with her?" Sterling demanded.

"I haven't done anything," Graves answered.

"She's not in our room."

"I haven't seen her. If you can't keep track of your wife, don't blame it on me." There was a long pause. "Didn't she say she was going to leave you?"

"How would you know that?"

Graves gave a nasty little laugh. "You two were talking about it loudly enough last night. If you want to have a private conversation, don't do it on the stairs."

Sterling cursed.

Then Graves raised his voice. "If you put your hands on me, you big ox, you'll be sorry."

There was a long moment of silence. Then she heard footsteps moving off and she was left standing in the hall, thinking that in the past few days she'd picked up a lot of information from overheard conversations. Maybe she should do more lurking in the halls.

But not now. Now she wanted to see if she could find Troy's cousin—just to satisfy herself that the woman was all right. But if she didn't find Nola, that would prove nothing, she reminded herself. Nola might well have carried out her threat of the night before and left under her own power, which would mean her disappearance had nothing to do with Graves.

Recognizing that she was on the verge of hysteria, she dragged in a steadying breath, then let it out slowly. *One thing at a time,* she told herself. *You were going to look in the strongbox. Take care of that. Then you can figure out your next step.*

With a renewed sense of purpose, she hurried up the stairs, staying alert, trying to make sure nobody saw her. Too bad she didn't have a flashlight or know more about the route Troy had taken this morning. If she could move through the secret passages, she'd be sure she wasn't observed.

Still, she made it to Troy's room without mishap,

slipped through the door and locked it before quickly crossing the sitting room.

As she stepped into the bedroom, she went stock-still. She'd been thinking that while she was up here, it might be prudent to make the bed. But it was already made.

Had Troy come back here and taken care of that? Or had Mrs. Martindale or someone else been snooping around?

With a sigh, she turned to the closet and followed the directions Troy had given her a few hours earlier. Just as he'd said, there was a seam in the paneling of the wall on the right.

At least that was something he hadn't lied about, she thought with a snort.

Once she knew what she was doing, it took only a few moments to figure out how to press correctly on the wall. Still she felt a small sense of triumph when she heard a click then saw a panel slide to the side. Beyond it was a small, dark recess. When her eyes adjusted to the gloom, she saw the glint of dull metal.

Gingerly she reached in and hauled out a heavy, square box about a foot on each side. Carrying it to the desk, she sat, unlocked it and lifted the lid.

Inside were the items Troy had mentioned, the kind of stuff you'd expect to find in a safe-deposit box. Troy and Grace's marriage license. Birth certificates. Grace's death certificate, which Bree couldn't stop herself from reading. The cause of death was listed as drowning.

For long moments she sat there picturing the accident. Then she resolutely went back to the other papers in the box.

She smiled when she saw that Troy had put in two pictures that Dinah had drawn with pastels. One showed the garden bright with flowers with the headlands in the background and a blue sweep of ocean and sky. The other was of a little girl and her father working in the garden. The pictures were quite good for a six-year-old. Dinah obviously had considerable artistic talent.

But that wasn't what Bree focused on. The drawings showed Dinah and Troy at a happy time in their lives. Was that why he had put them in the strongbox—because things were so different now and he wanted to preserve a reminder of their life when things had been happy? And what was he planning when he disappeared for good? Was he planning to take Dinah with him or to abandon her? Probably the latter, since he'd made Bree promise to take care of his daughter.

She thought again about the way he'd sounded then. Panicked, upset. As she recalled those moments, her emotions softened. He wanted Dinah safe, and maybe he thought that leaving her was his only choice. Maybe he knew he'd be on the run, and if whoever was after him caught up, it would be a disaster if she were along. She decided to take that interpretation as she set the pictures aside and looked for something worth hiding. She found it under the deed to the house.

Troy's will. She couldn't bear to read it. Instead she dug farther and found some stock certificates. They were the certificates that went with the balance sheet she'd seen from Enteck. Bree shuffled through them. As far as she could see, they would have represented millions of dollars—before the company had gone belly-up. Now they were practically worthless.

Someone had sunk a lot of money into the failed company. When Bree looked at the name on the certificates, she gasped.

Helen London.

As she stared at the official-looking papers, she knew

the assumptions she'd made were wrong. These were Helen's stocks, which meant Helen—not Troy—had lost millions. Probably her whole share of the family fortune.

Bree rocked back in her chair, trying to wrap her mind around what she'd just discovered. In the first place, Helen had lied to her. At least by omission. She'd acted as though nothing had changed, as though she was still well off. But unless she had some hidden source of income, above and beyond her state department salary, this bad investment had done irreparable damage to Helen's finances.

Bree went back to the strongbox, looking for more information, and found several letters clipped together.

Her eyes widened as she read the correspondence between Troy and his sister. The letters were dated after Grace had died. Apparently Helen had sent the balance sheet from the accounting firm and the stock certificates to Troy, telling him she was broke and asking him to advance her money on her share of Ravencrest. He'd told her he didn't have a spare cent because Grace had sunk so much into house restoration, and he couldn't give her anything substantial until some of his savings certificates came due, which wasn't until next year.

Helen had come back with a proposal to put Ravencrest on the market. Troy had vetoed the plan. There had been some back-and-forth discussion, but Troy remained opposed to selling the property. The tone of the correspondence began politely, but by the end Helen in particular was unable to hide her anger. She warned Troy that if he didn't go along with her plans, he was going to be sorry.

The threats made Bree's throat close. Helen had told her she was worried about Troy, but in these letters she hadn't sounded worried about anyone but herself.

Bree got up, carried the box back to the closet and stowed it where she'd found it. It had been safe there for months; she had no reason to believe it would be found now. Once it was hidden again and the key was safely in her pocket, she paced back toward the desk.

She didn't want to think anything bad about Helen, her best friend over the years. But evidence was piling up, evidence that was impossible to ignore. For example, Helen had kept Bree and Troy apart by lying about losing touch with her.

Why? What was her motive once Grace was dead? And what else had she done? Bree thought about that. Helen had always been sweet to her, but there were people who had asked her why they were friends. She'd had the feeling they wanted to tell her something she didn't want to hear about Ms. London, so she'd always made it clear that she wasn't into gossip about her friend.

Still, some of Helen's schemes and grudges had made her uneasy. Like the time in college Helen had been angry at another girl in the dorm, Stacy Masters, and had started a campaign against her. As she'd watched the whole dorm gang up against Stacy, Bree had been glad that Helen's wrath wasn't directed at her. In fact, that had been an underlying element in their relationship. Bree had been careful not to make Helen angry because she understood the consequences.

But now it didn't seem as if she could avoid them. Helen was up to something. Some elaborate plot that was still unfolding. Was she working against Troy or had they made some kind of pact? And were they using Bree for their own purposes?

Her thoughts were interrupted by a noise outside—a high, frightened scream carrying above the constant sound of the waves. She rushed to the window, but she could see nothing.

Bolting out of Troy's room, she hurried to the stairs, then quickly descended.

Mrs. Martindale was standing in the front hall looking alarmed.

"Did you hear that?" Bree asked breathlessly.

"Yes."

"Something's happened outside." She started toward the door but was stopped by the housekeeper's hand on her shoulder.

"Don't go out there!"

"But somebody may be in trouble."

"And if they are, what do you think you can do? You're just a little bit of a thing."

Bree opened her mouth then closed it again. She didn't know how to answer because she had no idea who had screamed and why. If the edge of the cliff had given way, and somebody had fallen into the sea, then they should start some kind of rescue operation.

"Go up and make sure Dinah is all right," Mrs. Martindale said. "I'll find Graves and get him to search around outside."

The mention of the little girl galvanized her. If Dinah had heard that scream, she would surely be worried. And Graves was certainly better equipped to take care of an emergency on the grounds than either one of them.

Quickly she retraced her steps, feeling the housekeeper's gaze burning into her back as she climbed the stairs. When she reached the landing, Mrs. Martindale was still in the hall, watching, as if to make sure that the schoolteacher followed directions.

She gave a small nod, then turned and hurried down

the corridor, taking the route she and Dinah had walked
the first evening she'd arrived.

At the place where Graves had startled them, the curtains rippled, eliciting a small gasp from Bree.

"In here," a voice whispered. It was Troy.

Bree wanted to shout at him and to ask what the hell
he was up to this time.

Instead she took a quick look behind her to make sure
the housekeeper hadn't followed her up the stairs. Then
she pulled aside the curtains and saw a narrow opening
that she hadn't found the first time she'd searched. But
apparently she'd been right all along. Graves had disappeared through one of the hidden passageways. And now
Troy was using it.

She stepped inside, leaving the curtain open so that
she could see into the dim tunnel.

Troy was standing several yards from the entrance.

"What happened outside?" she asked, straining to see
his face.

"I think we just lost Abner Sterling."

"What?"

"I'll take care of Dinah," he said. "You go find out
what Martindale and Graves are up to."

Without waiting for an answer, he turned and disappeared through the opening to the hallway. Still in the
darkened passageway, Bree looked around and saw a narrow, winding set of stairs that led back to the first floor.
They were constructed at a sharp angle so that she had
to step carefully to keep from tumbling down.

Flattening her hand against the wall and trying to be
as quiet as possible, she made her way down and found
herself facing a blank wall.

Obviously there was some way to open it, but she

wasn't going to search around until she knew what was on the other side.

Several small holes let light into the darkened space where she stood. Moving closer, she peered through one and saw Mrs. Martindale standing at the sink, washing dishes as though cleaning up from breakfast was the only thing on her mind.

Well, that wasn't quite true, Bree decided. There was a tension in the woman's shoulders that made her movements jerky.

A noise outside had her looking up quickly. As Bree watched, the door flew open and Graves barreled into the room.

"Is he dead?" Mrs. Martindale asked, her voice strangely calm.

Bree stared at the woman who had seemed so friendly. She was using the same tone of voice she'd used to extol her hot cross buns.

"Yeah, I took care of him for you."

"Not for me!" the housekeeper objected.

He ignored her and went on. "Just like Nola. I got rid of the pair of them, the way you said. But I don't like it. That wasn't what you said we had to do."

"We didn't have any choice. Not after Nola found London's ring lying on the ground by his grave."

Bree struggled to hold back a gasp, but she must have made a sound because Graves whirled toward the panel where she was hiding.

"Someone's listening."

Chapter Sixteen

From her hiding place, Bree saw Mrs. Martindale look toward the secret door. It felt as though the woman could see right through it and see Bree hiding in the darkness. She tensed, ready to defend herself.

But instead of marching across the room, the housekeeper gave a harsh laugh. "You old fool, there's nobody's there. Who are you expecting? The ghost?"

"Yeah, the ghost. He's stalking us. Not the one from way back in the past. I don't believe in him. But I believe in London's ghost."

"Only in your imagination."

"You gonna explain all the strange stuff that's been going on around here?"

Mrs. Martindale had stayed where she was, but Graves stomped toward the panel where Bree was hiding. She felt frozen, yet somehow she managed to reach out and grip the handle in front of her. Graves was right on the other side of the barrier and she ducked her head so that when he looked through the small holes, he wouldn't see her eyes.

She could hear him working at the door, pressing and pounding, but she hung on to the handle with a strength born of desperation.

If she was interpreting the conversation correctly, this man was admitting to having murdered two people before breakfast. And if he found her, she was next.

Bree braced her foot against the door, exerting pressure as he tried to battle his way through.

"The damn thing's stuck. I'm going up and in the other way."

She struggled to hold back a whimper. If he went upstairs, he'd find the panel open. Then he'd come down and find her.

"You are not! I don't want you bothering that child and the schoolteacher. They're both afraid of you. And I don't have time for them now."

"I've been watching the teacher. She's been stickin' her nose in where it don't belong."

"Don't worry. I've got her so confused with all my lies that she doesn't know whether she's standing on her head or her feet. The first thing I said to her when she arrived was a lie. I told her I didn't know she was coming. And of course Miss Helen and I had worked it all out."

While Bree took that in, she heard Graves move away from the door. She sagged back, fighting the weak feeling in her chest.

"You have to keep your cool," the housekeeper said. "Helen will be here next week."

Again Bree's mind tried to grapple with what she was hearing. Helen was coming to Ravencrest? From Macedonia? Or was that another lie? As Bree struggled to assimilate that information, Graves continued.

"I know that. You told me often enough."

"Well, you go about your business, making sure the place is in top condition. We want the buyers she lined up to be impressed with what they see. Get out and fix up the gardens like you're supposed to do.''

Bree's mind was reeling. Helen was coming and she'd gotten buyers for the property. She'd said in her letters to Troy that she wanted to sell the house and land. He'd written back, strongly opposing the idea. So she'd had her brother murdered to get him out of the way.

At least she'd thought she had him murdered, because Troy was only pretending to be dead. Lord, that had to be true, since the alternative was unthinkable, impossible. She'd seen Troy only a few minutes ago. He'd made love to her last night.

Her mind was working overtime to explain what had really happened to Troy. He'd been wandering around the estate with amnesia and a concussion, hiding, scaring people. But his memory was coming back. When he'd been injured, his mind had developed special powers.

Even as explanations whirled in her head, she was still listening to the couple in the kitchen, thinking that if she only had a tape recorder, she could nail them for murder. Not of Troy. But of Abner and Nola Sterling.

"I don't see why she had to hire that teacher," Graves was saying. "The woman's just a complication."

"Yes, but we need her to keep the school board off our back since we had to move up the timetable. We need her so everything here looks nice and normal until the sale goes through. And when she disappears, it will be easy enough to say that she's gone back east."

The breath froze in Bree's lungs and her hand clenched on the door handle. Oh, Lord, it sounded like they were planning to kill her, too.

"We didn't need the Sterlings," Graves said.

"Who else are we going to pin London's murder on?"

"Yeah, well, now they're dead, too."

"So they ran away. Or they were trying to run away, and they had an accident. We'll let Helen decide about that."

Graves made a sound of agreement then said, "I know you and Miss Helen are friends, but do you trust her? What if she turns around and stabs us in the back like she does everybody else?"

"Helen would never do that to me! We go way back. I worked here when she was just a girl. I was nice to her, sweet and kind, the way I am with Dinah."

Graves snorted.

"She trusts me. She knows I'm the one making this whole plan work."

"Just watch your back with her."

"You don't have to worry about me and her," Mrs. Martindale insisted, but this time she sounded a shade less positive. "Now go on, get to work."

"I don't like it when you boss me around. We're supposed to be partners," Graves muttered.

"I'm not bossing you," the woman denied. "I'm just trying to make sure that things look normal around here."

"Normal! Yeah, right. What are you going to tell the teacher when she asks why the Sterlings aren't around?"

"I'll tell her they decided to leave. Maybe the ghost scared them away." She cleared her throat. "Are the bodies in the sea cave?"

"Yeah."

"Then Helen can decide what to do with them. I vote for weighting them down and taking them out to sea."

"Weight them down! That will sure look like an accident."

"Not if you make certain they don't come bobbing up to the surface again."

Bree held back a strangled exclamation. The woman

had seemed so nice, but now she was showing her true personality. She must be some piece of work.

Bree heard the sound of water running, then footsteps rapidly leaving the kitchen.

Graves was going up to check on the entrance to the passageway!

Quickly she tiptoed back up the stairs, stepped into the hall and closed the panel. She was just starting toward Dinah's room when Graves walked around the corner of the hall. She made a startled sound.

"I didn't mean to scare you," he said, giving her a long look.

"No, of course not," she murmured, keeping her voice low and controlled.

"Just came up here to check something," he said.

"Well, I'm on my way to the classroom. I just had to stop and, uh, make a quick trip to my room," she answered, surprised that she could make her voice sound normal when she talked to him.

He stood in the hallway, waiting for her to leave, and she knew he was going to check the panel the minute she was out of sight. Thank the Lord she'd gotten out of the passage before he discovered her there.

Turning, she walked away, hurrying toward the schoolroom, where she found Dinah curled on the couch. She sat up and rubbed her eyes.

"I had another dream about Daddy. I haven't seen him in a long time, but in the dream he came here and hugged me."

Bree crossed to her and knelt beside the couch. "That's good," she said then asked, "What did he say in the dream?"

Dinah's expression closed up. "He said he has to go away. But he said you'd take care of me."

"I will," she murmured, knowing she had to reassure the child.

Tears glistened in the little girl's eyes. "I don't want him to go away."

"Neither do I," Bree answered, fighting her own tears.

"He told me to stay in here until you come back for me. He told me there's going to be a bad storm but I shouldn't be afraid, because nothing is going to happen to me." The child swallowed. "He says he needs to talk to you. He says to meet him out in the grove."

"When?"

"Now, I think."

For a moment Bree thought about taking the girl with her. But Troy had been very explicit in his instructions. She gave Dinah a quick hug, then slipped out of the room and headed for the back stairs, keeping an eye out for Graves or Mrs. Martindale.

Outside, she hurried through the gardens, then strode onto the headlands. Dark clouds were gathering in the sky and the wind from the ocean whipped back her hair as she hurried along the path, wondering where Graves had caught up with Nola and then Abner.

Angling toward the grove, she crossed the last open stretch and stepped among the trees.

Immediately she felt the familiar deep vibration and she saw the whirlwind pick up, gathering more and more leaves and other debris as it swirled between the tree trunks.

She held her breath, waiting, then sighed a mixture of relief and anxiety as Troy stepped out of the debris.

She ran to him, clung to him, reassured by the solid feel of his body even as she began to speak in a strangled voice. "I heard Mrs. Martindale and Graves talking about murder. They say he killed Nola and Abner this morning.

They say it was part of a plan Helen concocted to sell the estate. They say—'' She stopped, struggling to get the words out. ''They say they killed you!''

His hands soothed over her back. He bent his head so that his lips could brush her cheek. ''It's so wonderful to hold you,'' he murmured. ''It was wonderful to make love with you.''

She tipped her head back, her gaze fierce as she met his eyes. ''Troy, stop it! Tell me the truth this time!''

She felt his deep sigh.

''I'm sorry. If I could go back and change things, I would.''

''Troy, what happened to you?''

He began to speak, gathering force as he went. ''At first I didn't really remember. Then I didn't want to remember. But it's all there now. All the nasty details. I had a fight with Helen about the property. She bought that damn Enteck stock after I told her to stay away from it. She didn't need the money. But I know why she bought it. She wanted to have more than I did. Everything was always a contest with her. Sibling rivalry like you can't imagine.''

She gripped his shoulders, needing to hang on to him as she waited to hear the rest of it.

''Then she lost everything and she came to me, wanting to sell this property, the only big estate left on the coast up here. I'd sunk the past seven years of my life into this place and I wasn't going to just walk away from it. When I said no, I knew she was angry. I didn't realize how far she'd go to get back at me.

''After that Edith Martindale came back looking for a job. I hired her to take care of Dinah, but I didn't know that Helen had sent her here. Foster Graves was already working on the estate. Apparently, it wasn't difficult to play on his sense of disenfranchisement. He felt like he took care of Ravencrest, but I got all the benefits. Well, I worked here, too! I worked damn hard to supply the money Grace needed to make this house into the showplace she wanted for a home.''

''But what happened to you?'' Bree interrupted.

''That scene I showed you. I know now it wasn't the Sterlings. It was Martindale and Graves. I started thinking they were up to something so I set a trap for them. At dinner I was talking to Dinah about Aunt Helen, about how she used to leave valuable papers in the bedroom where you slept because that was a room she liked to use when she was here. But I said I kept forgetting to look for them, so I wanted Dinah to remind me after lunch the next day. Then I went out sailing. Only I doubled back and took the passageway to the room.

''I found Graves there. I didn't know Martindale was with him. She hit me over the head with a vase. While I lay there unconscious, I heard them talking. They had planned to kill me all along, but not so soon. Not until after Helen got back to the States. So I messed up their timeline. They couldn't have me dead yet, so they pretended I was still alive.''

She only half heard what he was saying. Instead she gave him her own version of the story. ''Yes, they hit you over the head and you had a concussion. You lost your memory. You were wandering around the estate—coming in through the tunnel and scaring Martindale and Graves.''

He sighed. ''I don't think that's true. I think they killed me and took the evidence out here.''

He looked over his shoulder toward the grave, and as she followed his gaze, her whole body began to tremble.

Her knees buckled, but he gathered her to him, lending her his strength.

She pressed her hands to his back, feeling his strong muscles and solid form under her hands.

Desperately she clasped him to her. "No! That can't be right. Not now." She rushed on, all logic fleeing her brain as she hurried to tell him what she was feeling. "Troy, I love you. I've loved you for so long. When you were married, I knew it was wrong and I tried to tell myself it wasn't true. But now there's nothing bad about those feelings. Please, you can't leave me now."

"Bree," he choked. "I love you, too. I fell in love with you that summer, and then I tried to put you out of my mind because I had a duty to Grace. But you were always there."

"Oh, Troy." She had longed to hear him say that. Tightening her hold, she cleaved to him with all her strength.

For a moment he held her just as tightly. Then he eased away so that his eyes could meet hers.

"I don't just use the tunnels," he said, his words clear but almost toneless. "I appear and disappear around the estate. I step out of that whirlwind of leaves. I call up storms."

She dug her fingers into his forearms as she struggled to give them both another explanation. "When you were hit on the head, you developed special powers. Don't tell me you're not alive. Don't tell me you're not real. I can feel your warm skin. Your solid body. Your mouth on mine."

As she spoke she clasped the back of his head and brought his mouth down to hers for a fierce, desperate kiss, pouring all her hopes and fears into it, trying with every cell of her body to deny his devastating words.

He kissed her with the same desperation, yet when he pulled back, his eyes were sad.

He stroked his hand gently along the line of her jaw. "I think Helen sent you here because she wanted to punish you."

"How could that be?" she objected.

"She saw us getting close that summer, and she resented it. She wanted you all to herself. She didn't want to share you with me. I think she asked you to come here now because she knew I loved you. Maybe in some twisted way she was thinking we'd be together."

"She…" Bree's voice trailed off. She'd been going to defend Helen. But she realized she'd never really known the woman. Helen had paid for her mother's operation, and she'd been so grateful. Now she could see the gesture differently. Maybe Helen had wanted to tie her to a sick woman so she wouldn't have a life of her own. It was awful to think of her friend's generosity that way, but once the idea took hold, it was difficult to shake it loose.

Troy was speaking again. "Helen didn't know what would happen when I started touching you, holding you, kissing you. Loving you. All those things made me as real and solid as I'm ever going to be. I wanted that. I wanted to be with you. Wanted to make love with you. But now I think we have to say goodbye."

"Troy, no. If you love me, you have to stay." Even as she pleaded with him, she couldn't deny the faulty logic of her words. Her love was strong. But he didn't have to stay, not simply because she loved him.

He was speaking again, low and urgently. "Will you take care of Dinah for me? My will made Helen Dinah's guardian. But I don't want Helen to get her hands on Dinah, especially since as my daughter she's my heir."

"You don't think Helen would harm Dinah."

"Yeah, I do. But I've written a codicil, dated six weeks ago, and put it in the strongbox with my other papers. You'll find it there. It names you as Dinah's guardian."

She stared at him, trying to take it in. But he rushed on.

"There's enough evidence in Mrs. Martindale's private papers for the police to arrest Helen before she sets foot on the grounds. After the storm you'll find those papers in her dresser drawer."

It sounded as though he was giving her final instructions, and the enormity of what he was saying made her numb.

"But most important, take care of Dinah for me."

Tears blurred her vision. "I will. Of course I will. But you'll be there, too."

He held her for a few moments longer. "Bree, before you came to Ravencrest, I was only a shadow, hardly there at all. My memories were dim. I didn't even know who I was. But you called to me. You brought me back to myself. Each kiss, each touch, made me more real, more solid. You couldn't even see me at first. But you changed that. You changed me. That first time I made love to you, that was the only way I could do it. But then you wanted more—and that's why I was able to give you more. You brought me back for a little while."

"No!" she choked. He was wrong. He had to be wrong. He had always been here. Just as he was now. Except for his memory.

HE TOOK HER BY THE SHOULDERS, set her a little away from him. "Don't make this harder for me. I need you to help me out."

"Anything!"

"Even with what you call my powers, I can't be two

places at once. I need you to go into the pantry off the kitchen. The main switch for the electricity is there. Flip it off. Then go to the schoolroom. Hold Dinah for me. Make sure she's not afraid. Do that for me, my love.''

''Yes.''

He pulled her back into his arms, clung with all the physical strength that had gathered within him since she'd arrived at Ravencrest. She was life, love, everything he had dreamed of over the long years of separation when he'd thrown himself into his work because he couldn't stand his marriage. Then she'd come back to him, but only for a little time.

''Go,'' he ordered, while he had the strength to send her away. ''And make sure Martindale and Graves don't see you.''

''Yes. All right.''

She was magnificent, he thought. Doing what he asked without hesitation.

Her coming here had made the difference for him. She'd pulled him out of his long lethargy, made him feel real and alive. And now she was making it possible for him to set the balance of things right.

He watched her run back toward the house. When she had disappeared from sight, he focused his attention elsewhere, calling up the wind and the storm clouds in preparation for his part of the drama that was going to be enacted here very soon.

BREE STUMBLED toward the house, tears choking her throat and blinding her vision. Desperately, she tried to outrun Troy's words.

They weren't true. They couldn't be true.

Not now. Not when the two of them had finally found each other again.

But deep in the secret, hidden part of herself, she couldn't deny his logic.

As she ran through the garden, the dark clouds grew more ominous in the sky.

It was going to storm, she thought with one part of her mind. Yes, a bad storm was brewing. Just as Troy had told Dinah.

As she reached the back door, she stopped and wiped her eyes, then pulled a tissue from her pocket. Troy had asked her to cut off the electricity. He had asked her to do it without Graves or Mrs. Martindale seeing her. Cautiously she approached the back door, then peeped in the window, looking for the housekeeper.

The kitchen was empty, so she opened the door and stepped inside, then took a moment to get her bearings. She'd never been in the pantry, but maybe it was on the other side of the room, behind the closed door.

She had almost reached the door when she heard footsteps behind her. Every muscle in her body froze. Then slowly, deliberately, she turned and found herself facing the housekeeper, who was looking at her with a dangerous expression on her wrinkled face.

"I went up to the schoolroom, but you weren't there. Now what are you up to?" Mrs. Martindale asked, her voice sharper than Bree had ever heard it.

For a moment her mind went blank. She felt like a kid who'd been caught hooking school. Only this was a lot more serious. If the housekeeper knew she was up to something, Graves might be called on to take care of the problem, the way he'd taken care of two other problems this morning.

As she stood there, struggling not to let her fear show, words popped into her mouth. Widening her eyes, she said, "I, uh, didn't get any breakfast, and I was hungry.

I was coming down here to look for some of those hot cross buns you mentioned. Isn't this the pantry?'' She gestured toward the door. ''I thought maybe I'd find them there.''

The housekeeper's tense expression eased. ''Yes, that's the pantry. But the buns are in the bread box.'' She crossed the kitchen, opened a metal box on the counter, and took out a plate with the buns.

''Could I have two?'' Bree asked. ''You made them sound so good.''

''Yes. Of course.'' Mrs. Martindale put two buns on a plate.

''And, uh, would it be too much trouble to get a cup of coffee?''

''No.'' The housekeeper filled a mug from the coffee-pot on the counter. ''Milk and sugar?''

''Just milk, thanks,'' Bree said politely, as though she had nothing more on her mind than her missed breakfast.

She pulled out a chair at the kitchen table, taking a bite of her bun, then a sip of coffee. Looking out the window, she watched the clouds darkening.

''It looks like a storm's coming up,'' she murmured as she sipped her coffee, keeping her head bent so that the anxiety she knew was on her face didn't show.

''Yes.'' She felt the housekeeper's gaze drilling into her and wondered how long she was going to stand there watching.

When the buzzer on the stove rang, they both jumped.

''Something in the oven?'' Bree asked, although she didn't smell anything cooking.

''No. I need to put the wash in the dryer.''

''Can I do it for you?''

''I told you once before you don't have to do my job.'' Without further conversation, the housekeeper turned and marched out of the room. Bree could hear her clomping down the stairs.

She stayed at the table for several moments, her tension gathering like the clouds. If the woman came back into the kitchen to check on her, she'd better be eating her bun and drinking her coffee. On the other hand, this might be her last chance to get to the electrical cutoff.

Swiftly she rose and hurried toward the pantry. Then she checked herself and turned to the cabinet where the housekeeper had stored the flashlight.

It was still there, and she snatched it up, her hand clamping around the hard plastic shaft as she pulled open the pantry door. It took only moments to locate the circuit box. The main switch was next to it.

Three things happened as she cut the power.

The room was plunged into gloom, a boom of thunder sounded above the house and from the floor below she heard Mrs. Martindale cry out, "The lights! The lights are out."

Bree was about to switch on the flashlight when the sound of heavy, running footsteps stopped her.

"Edith," Graves shouted. "Edith, are you all right?"

He pounded across the kitchen and Bree ducked back behind a set of shelves, just as he flung the door open.

"Edith? Where are you?"

Praying the darkness hid her, Bree pressed her back against the wall.

"Foster? I'm in the cellar. Help me. It's dark as pitch down here."

Graves turned and bolted toward the basement. Bree waited until she heard him clattering down the stairs before slipping out of the pantry. There was just enough light coming in the windows for her to find her way across the kitchen.

Below her she heard Mrs. Martindale crash into something then curse in a most unladylike fashion.

"Take it easy. I'm coming," Graves called.

"Did you bring the flashlight?"

"Uh, no."

"Go back and get it, you fool."

She heard him turn and start back to the kitchen, but she was already in the hall. She took the steps to the second floor two at a time. In the upper hall, she switched on the flashlight as she pounded toward the schoolroom.

When she dashed into the room, her heart leaped into her throat. She didn't immediately see Dinah. Then the beam of light revealed the child huddled in the corner clutching Alice.

Dinah whimpered and Bree called her name as she hurried across the room.

"The lights went out!" the girl said shakily.

"Yes, but it's okay. I've got the flashlight."

"I thought you weren't coming back. Mrs. Martindale was up here a little while ago, and she was looking for you. She was mad. I've never seen her so mad."

"She was upset," Bree murmured.

"I was scared of her. I wanted you to come back."

Bree hunkered beside the little girl and pulled her close. "I'm sorry I took so long. I think we're going to have a bad storm. So we'll stay here nice and snug until it's over. Okay?"

Dinah huddled against her. "Okay."

As the wind howled at the windows Bree held her close, needing Dinah's comfort as much as the child needed hers.

HE SENT A FORK of lightning across the sky. Then he wrapped the structure of the house in a gust of wind.

Bree had done what he'd asked without question, and now he was taking control of the drama.

He tugged dark clouds into place, then called down a torrent of rain from their depths.

As the storm raged outside, he went looking for Martindale and Graves. Bree had said he had special powers. He had hardly known how to use them at first. He had played tricks, small pranks. But he had felt his abilities growing. And now he knew his supernatural talents had come into their own.

He found Martindale and Graves in the basement, heard them stumbling around and gave them a nudge toward the steps.

They scrambled up and into the kitchen, where Martindale made her way across the tile floor and opened a cabinet, then cursed loudly.

"The flashlight. It's always here. But it's gone."

"I told you I couldn't find it! Maybe you have the wrong cabinet," Graves suggested.

"Of course not!"

In his best horror movie imitation, Troy sent his voice into the confines of the room. He had frightened these people before, frightened everyone in the old mansion. Now he multiplied that power, playing the part of an evil demon.

"Go, get out. Get off my property," he shouted, ending the instruction with a cackling laugh that reverberated in the air.

Then he punctuated the order with a sizzle of lightning along the kitchen counters and a thunderclap to match.

"Get out. Get out before it's too late."

The housekeeper screamed and pulled her apron over her head. She dashed out the door, Graves right behind her.

"I told you," he shouted. "I told you he'd get us."

"Quick, the truck."

They staggered toward the vehicle. But when Graves reached inside his pocket for the keys, his hand came out empty.

"The key's missing, too!" he screamed.

"What did you do, lose them, you fool?"

"I had them! They're gone. Don't call me a fool. You're the one who let Helen London talk you into this mess."

The wind swirled around them, howling its anger, tearing at their clothing and their hair, even as it confused their senses.

"Run!" Graves shouted. "Run for your life before he gets us."

Yes, run, Troy thought. *That's what I want you to do. Run.*

He tore at them with blasts of wind, blinded them with swirling fog. Pelted them with rain that drenched them to the bone.

Teeth chattering, eyes straining in the darkness, they staggered through the tempest, seeking safety.

He spun them around with a gust of wind, heard them gasp in terror as they lost all sense of direction. But he knew where they were at every moment. Near the cliffs. He used small bursts of wind to urge them closer, then closer still, to where he knew the ground was unstable.

Nature did the rest. The earth gave way beneath their feet and they plunged to the rocks below.

His night vision was excellent, and he watched them go over, heard their screams carried off by the wind.

He lingered for long moments, watching their bodies washing back and forth in the roiling waves.

His strength was fading now. He felt weak and shaky.

But he used the wind to sweep away the dark clouds and the rain before he turned his attention back to the house.

He knew his time on earth was almost finished. But he had to find Bree and Dinah to make sure they were all right.

He found them in the schoolroom, huddled together on the rug in front of the sofa. He wanted to go to them, to gather them both into his arms, to kiss them and stroke them and to tell them the danger was over.

Well, almost over. Helen was still at large. But he knew Bree would make sure she got what was coming to her.

"Troy?"

Bree must have sensed his presence.

He didn't answer and he didn't let them see him. He couldn't. Not now.

He didn't want to endure the sadness or the horror on their faces when they saw him fading like a light turned slowly down. The storm had taken all his energy and he could feel himself sinking into blackness.

He had been tied to this place because he had a job to do. And now he had done it.

It was over. Bree's love had brought him back to life, but only for a little time. He'd made love to her. Two glorious times. Not enough. Not nearly enough. But it would have to do.

Yet he understood what he had lost and the sadness of it gathered around him, choking off the last of his strength. He would never see his daughter celebrate her sixteenth birthday or marry the man she loved. He grieved for the loss of those precious events.

Nor would he ever hold the woman he loved again. It was too much to bear. With a trembling hand, he reached toward her and the child. But then his eyes misted and the image of them faded away and he was left in blackness.

Blackness that was somehow comforting. Blackness that smothered the terrible pain and soothed his wounded heart.

Chapter Seventeen

The wind died as suddenly as it had blown up, leaving an eerie quiet.

Bree stirred, standing and grasping Dinah's hand. For a moment she had thought Troy was here, but now it felt as if she and Dinah were the only two people at Ravencrest.

Troy had told her things—terrible things that she didn't want to believe. She forced them out of her mind because she couldn't break down weeping now. There was too much she had to do.

Yet she was cautious as she emerged from the schoolroom, taking Dinah with her. She clutched her small hand as they made their way down to the kitchen. It was empty, and the back door stood open. The wind had blown leaves and dirt inside.

"Mrs. Martindale will be angry about the mess," Dinah whispered as Bree closed the door.

"I don't think so," she answered as she crossed into the pantry and switched on the power, flooding the kitchen with light once again.

Dinah peered anxiously around. "I don't see Mrs. Martindale."

"I think she and Mr. Graves ran away," Bree murmured, suspecting that it was a little more than that. Above the sound of the wind she'd heard screams, long, vanishing screams like the sounds of people falling off a cliff. But she wasn't exactly going to talk about what might have happened outside.

Instead she got the child a hot cross bun and some milk, which she carried into the cozy sitting room next to the office.

"I'll be right next door," she said as she turned on the television and got a PBS channel.

Leaving the door open, she made sure that Dinah was comfortably settled in front of "Sesame Street," then worked at getting the lock off the phone.

As soon as the receiver was free, she called the Light Street Detective Agency.

Jo O'Malley, the woman who had started the agency, answered. When she heard who was calling, tension crackled over the line. "Bree, where have you been? We've been worried. We needed to get in touch with you, and you didn't leave a phone number."

She felt her chest tighten. The Light Street Detective Agency had been a wonderful place to work, and she knew now that she had let them down. "I'm sorry," she answered. "I thought I was being really clever. It turns out I can use some help. That is, if I'm not fired," she added in a small voice.

"You're not fired. Tell me what you need," Jo answered at once.

With a surge of gratitude, Bree lowered her voice and launched into an edited version of events, trying to keep the story coherent. She ended with the two recent murders and the disappearance of Graves and Martindale, whom she suspected were dead.

"It sounds like you've had a pretty scary time."

"Yes. And I'm not sure what to tell the police."

Jo paused for a moment then cut to the chase by asking, "You mean, what are you going to tell the police about Troy?"

Bree glanced into the other room, where she could see Dinah was still watching television. "I don't know what to say about him. I—" She stopped and started again. "I held him in my arms, and he seemed so real and solid. But he told me Martindale and Graves had killed him. And they thought so, too."

Jo was silent again, then said, "Do *you* think you were dealing with a ghost?"

The directness of the question stole the breath from her lungs. "I don't want him to be dead," she choked. "But…he said he had to go away. And, oh, Lord, Jo—" She gulped back a sob.

"I'm sorry," Jo said gently. "You care about him a lot, don't you?"

"Yes."

Jo's voice firmed. "But you have to be practical. You don't want this turned into a supernatural circus. And from what you said, it sounds like there's correspondence between Martindale and Helen about Troy's murder. Can you keep your cool and tell the police you haven't seen him since you arrived?"

Bree thought that over, yet she still couldn't abandon all hope. "But what if…"

"What if it turns out he has amnesia and is wandering around the estate somewhere?"

"Yes," she breathed.

"Then he won't have much to say, will he?"

Bree closed her eyes for a moment. Jo was giving her a way out of a very sticky situation. "I can do it," she murmured.

"Good." Jo's voice turned businesslike. "Just a minute. Let me check on something." She was gone for several minutes. When she returned she said, "Alex was on assignment in Portland. I caught him as he was leaving. He can be there in a few hours."

Bree breathed out a small sigh. Alex Shane, one of the detectives with the agency, was a good man to have on her side.

"Right now, call the local police and tell them a sudden storm blew up and you think there might have been an accident on the estate. You can't find the housekeeper or the handyman."

"Yes. Thanks," she answered.

"Or the Sterlings, for that matter. Don't volunteer anything else. Let them investigate and see what they find. And don't let them intimidate you. You haven't done anything wrong."

"Yes. Thanks," she said again.

As soon as the conversation ended, Bree called 9-1-1 and made the report.

TWO DAYS LATER a lot of the mess had been sorted out, thanks in large measure to Alex. A former police detective, he knew how to talk to the cops.

The authorities had found two bodies in the sea cave and two more bodies on the beach. And Bree had told her edited story several times.

When the police wanted to speak to Troy, she kept repeating that she'd heard Martindale and Graves talking about having killed him, and she hadn't seen him the whole time she'd been at Ravencrest. Dinah backed her up on the last part. She hadn't seen her father in weeks, except in her dreams. So Troy was presumed dead, although they didn't find his body.

One mystery Alex solved was the disappearance of her gun. He found the pieces scattered in the pit. So it had gone over the edge that first night, and she hadn't known it.

Also, with the information Troy had given her, she was able to find documentation of Helen's diabolical scheme. The correspondence he'd mentioned was in Martindale's dresser drawer where he had said it would be. Bree produced the strongbox with the stock certificates and the letters between Troy and Helen.

The whole plot was spelled out. The Sterlings had walked into the trap. They had been down on their luck and they'd been grateful when Troy had allowed them to stay. Then he'd disappeared and Mrs. Martindale had taken charge, telling them that if they wanted to stay, they had to act to the outside world as if they were running the estate.

Helen London was one more complication Bree didn't want to deal with. She was still too shocked and saddened by the elaborate and murderous scheme her supposed friend had cooked up. She'd thought she knew Troy's sister, or at least she'd ignored what she didn't want to know about her. That had been a mistake, and she'd almost paid with her life.

With the proof of Helen's scheme in hand, the authorities were waiting for her and she was taken into custody as soon as she set foot in San Francisco.

BREE HAD GIVEN her official statement to the police. But alone in bed at night, she went over and over the events of her week at Ravencrest and the events of the more distant past, trying to figure out what she could or should have done differently.

One decision she made was not to tell anybody about

the grave in the grove of trees. She didn't want them to dig it up and find a body buried there. Against all reason, she wanted to cling to the belief that Troy was still alive, although she had no idea where he was.

Several times she told Alex that she needed to go out for some air and slipped away. Really, while she made contingency plans to take Dinah back to Baltimore, she was searching everywhere for Troy. She knew she was being irrational, but now that she had the run of the estate, she explored the secret tunnels. She went through every room in the house. She even went out to the grove, praying she would meet up with him there as she had before. But he was in none of the places she looked. Each time she searched and didn't find him, she felt a new sense of loss weighing her down as though she were slogging through heavy snow.

As the days stretched on, a great sadness settled over her, so that it was often difficult to hold back her tears.

She'd loved Troy London all of her adult life. She'd finally gotten together with him again and found to her joy that he'd never forgotten her, either. But it had already been too late. Against her will, she had to accept what he had told her before the storm. Graves and Martindale had killed him, and the man she'd held and kissed had only been a ghost, a ghost who had been made more real and alive by his tie to her.

At least she had that knowledge. For a little while she'd been able to hold on to him through the strength of her feelings. But now it was finally time to cut the last tie with him.

Well, not the last. She had Dinah, his child, and Bree would raise her with all the love she had to give. Not just because she was Troy's daughter, but because Bree had already come to love the girl.

An hour before they were to leave for the airport, she made sure once again that everything Dinah needed was packed. Then she asked Alex to watch the little girl while she went outside for a while.

Alex gave her one of his long looks. She knew he was aware of her despair and her restlessness. She knew he had talked to Jo about what had really happened at Ravencrest. But Bree hadn't spelled it out to him in so many words, because talking about what she'd lost was simply too painful.

One last time she slipped out the back door and hurried through the garden to the headlands.

What a glorious location, she thought. Troy had loved this patch of seacoast. And she had come to appreciate the wild beauty of the setting.

Still, her shoulders sagged as she made her way through the tall grass and low bushes, feeling the wind tearing at her clothing and her hair. She had found him here and lost him here, and now she was coming to say goodbye. Finally. Because there was nothing left for her at Ravencrest. Still, her heart was pounding as she stepped into the shade of the grove and the power of the place caught and held her as it had on her first visit.

A bone-deep sadness shimmered through her.

"Troy," she murmured, unable to banish the tears from her voice. "If your spirit is here, I want you to know that I'll take care of Dinah for you. I love her. She's a wonderful child, and I think she'll be happy with me in Baltimore. When she's a little older, I'll let her make the choice of where she wants to live—here or back there."

She brushed away the moisture in her eyes and took a deep breath, then began to speak again. "Troy, I love you. God gave us a little time together, and I'm so grateful. I just want you to know that.''

There was no answer. She had given up expecting one. As she stood in the twilight grove, her tears flowed out of control. It was time to leave, time to abandon hope. Rationally, she knew that as she wiped at her cheeks with the backs of her hands, then fumbled for a tissue in her pocket. The last thing she wanted was for Alex to come out and find her crying.

Still, something held her in this place. As she lingered, she realized she felt the way she had that first night when Troy had come to her bed.

The sense of anticipation clogged her throat, made it difficult to take in a full breath. When she felt a slight tremor of the ground below her feet, her heart stopped, then started up again in double time.

From deep within the earth came a subtle vibration, a humming that she remembered so well from other times she had ventured here. The air around her seemed to dim and thicken, and the humming of the earth swelled.

She felt suspended in time, suspended in a world that was not her own, where the laws of nature were different from this earth.

Her heart began to pound as she realized that something else was happening. Like that first time she had come here. She felt it deep in her bones, in her soul. In her heart.

A dozen yards away pine needles rustled and then flared away from the ground in a sudden updraft.

Transfixed, Bree watched the debris swirl in a spiral pattern, then whip away among the trees. The circle of wind gathered speed and force like a cyclone collecting more and more swirling matter. She had seen Troy step out of the cyclone here in this grove. But sight was impossible now. She had to squeeze her eyes shut to protect them as the air howled around her head like a human cry of agony—or triumph.

She could hear the wind gathering force, tearing at the tree branches, and real fear shot through her. She was rooted to the spot, until the swirling mass of debris caught her in its grasp and spun her around, making her lose all sense of direction as she struggled to stay on her feet.

Dizzy, disoriented, she reached out a hand, groping for a tree trunk, as she tried to steady herself. For a terrible moment her hands clutched at nothing, and she thought the wind might fling her out of the grove and over the cliff.

Then she felt something solid, and grasped for purchase. It wasn't tree bark she felt. Not at all. Instead her fingers closed around flannel fabric.

"What—" Her exclamation ended in a gasp as she was pulled tightly against a man's hard body.

"Troy?" she breathed, unable to see him in the whirling vortex, unable to believe that the unbelievable was happening.

By some miracle, could this really be him? Or was this whole episode just some trick of her fevered imagination? Some fantasy she'd conjured up out of her own pain because she wanted him so much, and she couldn't bear the idea of living without him.

He held her more tightly as the wind rocked them, pressed them together, and then whipped away, leaving the tree branches trembling in its wake.

Breathlessly, she waited for the illusion to fade away, but his body stayed real and solid against her. And she dared to let the tiny kernel of hope inside her grow and bloom.

Cautiously, she tipped her head up and opened her eyes, then blinked as his tanned face and windblown hair filled her vision.

She gasped, her hands clenching and unclenching on his shoulders. The whirlwind had vanished, but Troy was here. Troy was holding her in his embrace.

She breathed his name, then said it more loudly as she clasped him to her, trembling as a great swell of relief and shock washed over her—even when her mind still questioned if this was reality or only her desperate longing.

"Bree." He sounded as astonished as she felt. And as he whispered her name, his arms banded around her.

She pressed her face to his chest, breathing in the spicy scent of his body, then raised her face to stare at him. "How... Where did you come from?"

He blinked and looked around in wonder, then reached to pluck a strand of moss from her hair. "I don't know. I was somewhere dark and cold, then the wind grabbed me up and brought me here."

Her fingers dug into his arms as she struggled to take in what had happened—what must have happened. "Oh, Troy... You're here. You're here!"

For long moments they clung together, holding each other, touching, their lips brushing, clinging, then breaking apart again so that they could gasp out each other's names. Tears blurred her vision again, but now they were tears of joy.

He brushed a drop of moisture away with his knuckle. "Don't cry. I'm here."

"I know. Oh, I know," she answered, finally daring to believe it was true.

She dragged in a breath and struggled for coherence.

"What's the last thing you remember before the dark place?" she asked.

"I remember the storm."

She nodded tightly.

"Then I came to the schoolroom to say goodbye to you and Dinah."

"We didn't see you."

"I didn't let you see me."

She grasped him more tightly. He was so real, so solid, yet he had felt that way to her before. Only this was different, she suddenly realized with a sense of relief. The look in his eyes was different. Always before he'd looked as if he was gazing at her from a far distance. But not now.

There were questions she didn't want to ask. But she needed answers. "You told me you were a ghost," she murmured.

He dragged in a breath and let it out slowly. "Maybe I was. I remember I felt so numb, so disoriented." He reached up to gingerly touch the back of his head. "I guess it has something to do with this big lump back here."

Carefully she reached up and found the spot, feeling the injury. "You were hurt."

"Yeah. I think I lost my memory for a while. Then I saw you at Ravencrest, and when I came to you, I started remembering stuff. Not everything at first, but bits and pieces." She saw him swallow. "The first thing I remembered was how much I wanted you. Then I remembered it was more than that. It was love."

"Oh, Troy." She still didn't understand what had happened. He'd shown her what he said was Troy London's grave. But maybe he'd only thought that was true. Or maybe God had given him a second chance to come back and love her.

She'd been sure that he was lost to her forever. Now she had him back, in her arms, and she would keep him for whatever time she was allotted. When he bent his head and kissed her with a fierce possessiveness, she kissed him back.

He hugged her to him, rocked her in his arms. "I want you."

"Yes," she answered as he bent to press his face to the tops of her breasts. "But not now. Not out here."

"Why not?"

"Because I have a plane reservation. And my friend Alex will come looking for me if I don't go back to the house."

"Alex? You've got a friend here named Alex?" he asked, his voice suddenly sharp.

"Yes. A happily married man. He came to Ravencrest to help me take care of things. Like showing the police where to find the bodies of Mrs. Martindale and Foster Graves. And like making sure your sister was arrested the minute she set foot in San Francisco."

She felt him stiffen.

"Do you know how Mrs. Martindale and Graves died?" she asked.

"I think they fell over the cliff in the storm."

"Yes. A convenient accident," she murmured.

He nodded gravely. "We're rid of them now." For a long moment his eyes were focused toward the ocean, then swung back to her. "It's a miracle. You came back to me."

"I think it's the other way around, but we won't argue about it." As she spoke she slid her hands possessively over his back, his shoulders, unable to get enough of the feel of him under her fingertips.

"I loved you when you were a college girl. I love the woman you've become."

"Thank you," she whispered.

He framed her face with his hands. "Oh, Bree, let's not waste any more time. We've lost seven years. I don't want to lose seven more hours with you. Marry me and live here with me." He stopped. "That is, if you like Ravencrest enough to live here."

"I love it."

He gathered her close. "You're wonderful with Dinah. You'll make a wonderful mother for her."

"And our other children," she supplied.

"Yes."

"Of course I'll marry you. I've loved you for so long. I thought I couldn't have you. But everything's changed."

"Yes, everything," he agreed. Then his face turned serious. "Money is going to be tight for a while."

"I know. I read your letters to Helen. But I don't mind. I could live on bread crumbs if it's with you."

He laughed. "Things aren't quite that bad."

He slung his arm around her shoulders and they started back to the house.

"What am I going to tell Alex?"

He laughed. "That you're not going back to Baltimore, after all."

"What do I tell him—and everybody else—about you?"

He thought for a moment. "That I had amnesia. That I was pretty out of it for a while. But your coming here made all the difference. Your love made all the difference. You brought me back to myself."

She squeezed his hand, and he knit his fingers with hers. Everything had changed, and she was still trying to catch her breath. But she clung to one momentous reality. The man she loved was with her.

They were walking fast now, hurrying toward the house. "Dinah will be so glad to see you," Bree said. "I can't wait to see her face when we walk in."

"Yes." He laughed again. He was doing that a lot, and she sensed the freedom in him.

"Yes," he said again, and this time it was an affirmation. "The three of us are a family now. Right from this moment on."

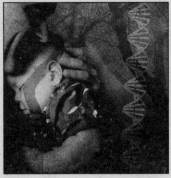
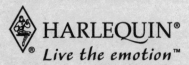

The world's bestselling romance series.

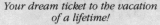
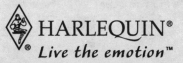

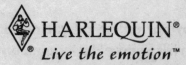